STEALING
CHILI RELLENO

A TONY TAYLOR ADVENTURE

BOB MEANS

High Tide
Publications, Inc.

It's never too late to write

Deltaville, Virginia

Published by High Tide Publications, Inc.
www.Hightidepublications.com

Thank you for choosing this authorized edition of *Stealing Chili Relleno.*

At High Tide, our mission is to discover, promote, and publish the work of talented authors over 50. Your support by purchasing an authorized copy is crucial in helping us bring their work to you.

Your support in our mission to bring the work of our authors to a wider audience is deeply appreciated. Thank you for choosing to purchase an authorized edition.

Edited by Carol J. Bova.

Book design by Firebellied Frog Graphic Design
www.Firebelliedfrog.com

CHAPTER 1

I come from a wealthy and liberal San Francisco family. In my high school days, I was considered a wayward youth running around town causing trouble as a member of Lefty Jackson's street gang. Our biggest accomplishment was climbing to the top of the Golden Gate bridge on a foggy night without getting caught. Whenever I see the bridge now, I think about it being the first of the many unlikely adventures I've survived.

On that night, I stared up at the giant orange suspension cable from the base on the north side of the Golden Gate Bridge. It was foggy, but warm enough that I didn't have to zip up my black leather jacket.

"Tony, this was your idea, so you lead the adventure!" Lefty insisted.

Desperate Chances was a game Lefty invented. Gang members in our last year of high school took turns producing wild and crazy ideas to challenge the rest of us in a test of bravery. The best idea was to climb the Golden Gate Bridge's main cable to the top.

I thought of it when I noticed men working on the bridge cables. The thirty-six-inch diameter galvanized steel wire cables went to the top of the towers, 500 feet above the roadway and 746 feet above the water. It took planning, but Lefty and I worked out the details. To avoid getting arrested, we planned the challenge for a foggy night. We had no intention of climbing sober.

The perfect night arrived; a thick fog lay over the bay, and there was barely a wisp of wind. A drunken sailor bought us three six-packs of beer. We chugged three beers each, and we felt unduly brave. Even so, before we started the ascent, we drank another.

Nothing could stop us now.

We worked our way up, stanchion by stanchion, with a length of rope tied around our waists to secure us to the cable's handrail. Each of us carried a can of beer in our back pockets.

I led the way, looking straight ahead as I heard Lefty's breathing behind me. Above the fog, an increasingly solid and chilly breeze revealed a bright, starry night. I stopped to look around, gazing at the top of the bridge, when I heard someone retching behind me.

"Oh, God, Mike! Did you have to vomit right on the cable?" a half-hysterical voice screeched in the darkness. "How the hell am I going to get past that?"

"The question is, how are you gonna get past ME! I gotta get down from here!" came another voice.

A slight wave of panic passed through me as I concentrated on the goal, which was still far above. Lefty took control behind me.

"Anybody who chickens out now is out of the gang! You can rely on it! Quit your bitching and keep climbing!"

The higher we climbed, the colder and windier it became. I wished I'd zipped up my leather jacket at the bottom. It was warm below, and I felt a slight sweat then, but now, my flapping jacket whipped a cold metal zipper across my face. I dared not let go of the safety rails lest I fall to my death, either on the road or in the unforgiving water below.

I finally reached the top and climbed onto the tower platform, encouraging the others. They joined me at the top, and the shouting became a raucous celebration. Our bursting bladders christened our extraordinary feat as we stepped close to the platform edge and whizzed into the night air. Mike faced directly into the wind, wearing much of his recycled beer on his Levis and boots. We reached into our back pockets and finished off the celebratory beers.

I spotted an unlocked hatch and pulled it open to find a narrow set of stairs spiraling down the inside of the tower. Pitch black, I flicked on the flame of my lighter, revealing a bottomless pit. The others followed as I climbed down the stairs.

Strange sounds came from inside the tower. One of our voices complained about feeling suffocated in the long, tight, dark enclosure.

We reached the bottom and didn't find anything of interest except our pride for accomplishing the great feat and didn't linger.

We hurried back to the top, laughing all the way. Although we were tired, we still had to go down the cable.

Back in the night air, the cold began to set in. Completely in awe, I saw the stars in the otherwise dark sky around me. The other bridge tower peaked above the fog, a surreal vision as I stood on top of the world between the stars and the clouds.

Lefty, wanting a last act of celebration at the tower's peak, reached behind him and pulled out a pistol. He began firing into the air, its blasts visible for miles around. He scared the hell out of everyone! Mike jumped back and would have fallen to his death had we not grabbed and pulled him to safety.

A small aircraft flew over the bridge and circled back. Spotted, we wasted no time heading down the cable. I led the pack.

Why was it easier going up than down, I wondered? Halfway there, before descending into the fogbank, my foot hit something slick, and I slid off with a blood-curdling scream. Expecting to meet death somewhere below, I was stopped with a painful jerk as the loop of rope around my waist slid up to my armpits, where I dangled in the darkness.

"Oh, God! Oh, God!" I screamed as hands pulled at my jacket, my hair, my arms, anything they could grasp to pull me back up onto the smelly cable.

This massive adrenaline rush sobered us up as we were desperate to get down before the police could greet us at the bottom. We made it to our cars in time to escape the passing of the flashing lights of police cars and an ambulance going in the opposite direction, too late to catch us.

CHAPTER 2

When I graduated from high school, my parents gave me an opportunity. They offered to financially support me until I found my way if I didn't feel ready to continue my education. I chose life experiences, a choice that led me to nightly wanderings where I met Janet LeGrand, a woman twenty years my senior. Janet, a wealthy art dealer and gallery owner, and I had a mystical attraction the first time we met. She took me as her lover, which I didn't mind at all.

Janet introduced me to Bohemian culture, where I frequented dimly lit clubs, listened to poetry and jazz, and discussed philosophy. I didn't know much about philosophy, but after wine and a reefer, I could fake it, as could the other untried minds sitting with me.

It started one night when Janet and I sat at the Q Club, a back-alley Bohemian club in North Beach. Finding the Q Club was only possible if one knew where to look. That's where Janet introduced me to Brian. I didn't know it then, but Brian and Janet were members of a secret culinary society.

Brian lived on a houseboat in Sausalito, one of thirty moored together north of the town marina. When I mentioned I needed a place to stay, he told me of a houseboat available for rent.

"It's three slips down from mine," he added.

I arched my eyebrows. Sausalito was an artist's dream, an avant-garde paradise, the most excellent place on the bay. I never dreamed I'd land a place there.

"Could you tell me about it?"

"The owners are going to Baja for the winter and want to rent it out for six months. They're asking $150 a month."

I sat silently and thought that, for a 19-year-old kid, six months was a lifetime. The price was well within my budget. I was riding high on this new and exciting life, utterly oblivious to any plans Janet and Brian might have for me.

With the music playing, I searched for a way to improve my chances of getting into this houseboat.

I summoned the courage to ask Brian, "Do you work here in San Francisco?"

He perked up, "Yes, I'm a chef."

Responding foolishly, "A cook?"

"No," he smiled. "I'm a chef."

I lifted my glass for another swig of wine, "One fifty a month?"

"Yes," answered Brian.

"Do you mind if I come to look at it tomorrow?"

"Not at all, but it's not up to me. You'll have to talk to the owners."

"What time?"

"No later than nine. I must get to work."

"I'll be there."

The following day, I drove across the Golden Gate Bridge before nine. I arrived an hour early, excited about having my place—a houseboat! I remembered Brian's directions and found the one available. I counted on Brian to introduce me and help close the deal. The houseboat looked great, and I couldn't wait to look inside.

Three houseboats up, Brian sat on his deck reading the morning paper.

When I approached him, he looked up. "I figured you'd be here early. Would you like a cup of coffee?"

He motioned me to sit, and he brought the coffee. I took my first sip when he prodded, "Fill me in. What's up with your life?"

I mentioned my parents, freedom, and desire to explore the world before committing to anything long-term.

He listened intently, "What do you like to do?"

"I used to get off on hanging around Lefty Jackson and his street gang, but now that I met Janet, I dig the clubs, especially being with her and her friends at the Q Club discussing stuff. But, before I can do anything, I hope this works out."

"No problem. I talked to Megan and Carl earlier, and they'll happily rent you their place. Drink up, and we'll go over and close the deal. Then you're on your own. I have to get to work."

Brian knocked on the houseboat door. I recognized the man who came out. I'd seen him in clubs.

"Carl, this is Tony."

"Tony, nice to meet you. I've seen you around. You're interested in our home, are you?"

"Yes, I am," I stammered.

Carl's wife, Megan, peeked around the door, "Hi Tony. I'm Megan. Nice to finally meet you. I've seen you at the clubs. Who'd have thought you'd be renting our place? Come on in."

As a rule, houseboats are compact. This one had skylights that filtered natural light onto green potted plants hanging from the ceiling. A nude painting of Megan was above the bookshelf. Dark wood paneling continued into the open kitchen with redwood countertops and blue tiled backsplash. Above the deep porcelain sink, a large porthole swung out on bronze hinges. A small hallway terminated in a bathroom with enough room for the toilet, sink, and showerhead flowing onto the tiled floor and walls. The bedroom accommodated a double bed with lighted side tables.

Brian interrupted the tour, "You guys get to know each other. I have to get to work."

After we said goodbye to Brian, Megan asked, "Do you like it?"

It was so cool, I blurted out, "Like it? I love it! What do I have to do to move in?"

I spent an hour with Carl and Megan, getting to know one another, and I gave them the first and last months' rent. It was a loose deal, with Megan's genuine concern: "Don't burn the place down, and please don't kill my plants."

Before they left for Baja, we agreed to meet at the Q Club on Friday night. When I returned home to my parents, I mentally sorted out what to bring.

Friday night came, and I eagerly showed up at the Q Club at nine o'clock. I liked Carl and Megan. They were giving me my first break in life. Waiting for them to arrive, I sat back, listening to a poetry recital.

They came through the door at 10:15, and my planned nonchalance melted as I stood and waved them to my table. Megan looked up and moved my way. She hugged me and kissed my lips. Carl squeezed my shoulder as they sat down.

"Have you been here long?" Megan asked, ordering drinks.

"Just got here," I lied.

The reader finished his poem and made way for a small jazz combo. The server brought our drinks. That allowed us to talk between acts.

"How long have you known Brian?" Megan asked.

"I met him a couple of weeks ago."

"Then you're not his lover?"

Set back by the question, I said, "No, I'm not gay! I didn't know he was."

"Yes," Megan continued, "He is an incredible guy. He's so talented at cooking that he travels worldwide as a featured chef."

"I didn't know that. He said he was a chef when I met him, nothing more."

"If you're interested in creative food prep, since you'll be neighbors, he might show you some of his tricks... I mean cooking tricks, that is," she laughed.

I looked down at the table and nervously joined the laughter.

The night continued with music and reading interspersed with short conversations. At two in the morning, I was ready to head home. I left after getting another kiss from Megan.

As I drove toward home on Telegraph Hill, I couldn't shake Megan's comment about Brian, which caught me off guard; I wondered how to deal with his sexual orientation. I liked Brian, thought he was interesting, and wanted him as a friend, with no desire to have sex with him. Also, I'd never thought much about culinary arts, but now that it had been brought to my attention, it sparked my interest.

CHAPTER 3

I woke late the following day and wondered what to do for the next week and a half before moving into my new place. A phone call from Janet turned my thoughts around. She was going to Boulder Creek for three days to stay at her brother's cabin and wanted to know if I wanted to come along.

I liked being with Janet, even though we were different ages. She was a nudist, which was very cool. A full-bodied woman, not fat, Janet was more than attractive. I didn't have to think long before saying, "Yes!"

When I asked if we'd be alone, she answered, "Mostly. But make sure you bring a nice shirt and tie with long pants. There will be an evening gathering. I'll be there to pick you up at three this afternoon."

Janet drove up and honked the horn of her 1950 brown Hudson. I entered the passenger side and threw my small bag in the back. I knew it would be warm in Boulder Creek, so I didn't bring much. Janet would be naked.

"How're you, Sweetie?" Janet asked as I slid in.

"Great! But I can't wait to move into my new place."

"Isn't it exciting? Your first place and such a cool one at that! Brian told me you got it."

"Brian helped. It wouldn't have worked without him. How well do you know Brian anyway?"

"Pretty well. I've known him for five years. He and I have done a couple of projects together. I met him not too long after he moved out from Illinois. The guy's fantastic! Don't know how he produces his recipes.

It blows me away."

I was confused when Janet said they had worked on a couple of projects together, so I asked the obvious.

"What kind of stuff does he cook?"

"Cordon Bleu, exotic Mediterranean tastes, with great Asian dishes, and produces his own recipes. Being his next-door neighbor, you'll see."

During the two-and-a-half-hour drive, we talked like a couple of hens. We always had fun together.

It was hard to imagine Janet was only a couple of years younger than my mother. Although they were both women of means, they were not from the same planet!

Months ago, I was that boy who had proven my strength by climbing the Golden Gate Bridge. Thanks to Janet, I was no longer that fumbling boy trying to cop a feel from some flirtatious yet timid girl. I also was not drooling in my bedroom next to Lefty over a spread of half-naked African women in *National Geographic Magazine*. Now, all that seemed so long ago, I was a MAN, completely swept off my feet by a real WOMAN, getting ready to move into my own houseboat in Sausalito! Life was beyond anything I'd ever imagined!

I couldn't help but wonder what attracted Janet to me. I wasn't any kind of a he-man, only five foot nine and with a ruddy complexion. But she flattered me by saying I had a good build and was a quiet thinker, making me mysterious and confident. She said it made me seem older than my age. That was good enough for me! I could never have imagined the plans she had for me.

Janet LeGrand told me she grew up in the avant-garde art world. She loved her parents and loved working with them, especially as she got older. When her parents moved to San Francisco to expand their art business, Janet took the opportunity to stay with relatives in France to study art. Once home, she inherited the family business when her parents were tragically killed in a car accident returning from a gala in Sacramento.

She'd married a couple of times, and at forty, she savored her freedom and tried to stay young. I met her criteria for that.

After the drive to Boulder Creek, we zigged and zagged up a curvy road. I was excited to spot the two-story cedar-sided lodge for the first time.

I must have been gaping at its sight because Janet laughed, "Come on, let's go in."

I reached for my bag and followed her to the porch as she fumbled for her keys to unlock the door. It was five o'clock, with summer daylight left.

The entryway glistened with varnished hardwood floors. Through an open double door to the right was the formal dining room. To the left, the staircase led up to the bedrooms. The entry hall opened to a large room with Turkish rugs, an oversized, comfortable leather couch, overstuffed chairs, and end tables. On one wall was a huge rock fireplace, and opposite was the open kitchen. The side wall next to the kitchen had a fully stocked wine rack. The main attraction was the view through three French doors onto a large deck overlooking the creek.

Janet tossed her bag on the couch, "Come out here, and let me show you this."

I followed her to the deck. She perched on the railing and pointed at a bridge crossing the creek. In the middle of the bridge, a mythical-looking redwood teahouse with redwood split shakes for roofing stood.

"Do you like that?" she asked.

I gazed at the teahouse, then at her, lost for words. I smiled and nodded.

Janet took my arm, "Come on, I'll show you upstairs, but first we need to open some wine."

She selected and opened a bottle of Merlot. "Come on, Tony. You haven't said anything since we arrived. What do you think?"

"I'm amazed with the setting here. I never imagined. Your brother built the tea house over the creek."

"He did. Here, have a drink."

She took a couple of quick drinks, "Get your bag. Let's go up."

The top of the stairs had a bathroom with bedrooms on either side. Paintings hung on the wall along the stairs. We turned to the bedroom on the left, and she took my hand and pulled me in.

She stood next to the double bed facing the creek window, threw her bag on the bed, set her glass on the side table, looked at me, and disrobed as I watched.

Naked, she picked up her wine, took a drink, and moved toward me.

She held her glass in the air and held me tenderly by the back of the neck, then planted a big kiss on my lips. I dropped my bag, and my left hand fondled her bottom while the kiss lingered.

She broke the kiss by saying, "Take your clothes off, and we'll take the bottle to the teahouse and finish it."

I couldn't comply fast enough. Janet reached the head of the stairs and paused to take another drink. My excitement began to grow as I unzipped and dropped my pants to the floor.

Out on the deck, stairs led to the wooden path toward the base of the bridge. She stood naked on the bridge, and I gazed at her. She was beautiful and without tan lines.

My skin was freckled. I didn't tan so beautifully, but Janet looked at me as if I were an Adonis. Of course, I had to believe her!

She entered the teahouse and yelled, "Grab another bottle of Merlot before you come down."

I returned to the wine rack and found another bottle of Merlot. Janet had finished the first bottle before I entered the teahouse. She sat on a large pillow propped up on the corner post, her legs crossed at the ankles.

Upstream, the water rushed over a rock outcropping. Janet's brother built a small dam downstream, creating a five-foot-deep pool directly under the teahouse. It was five thirty, and the air was warm enough to form beads of sweat on my forehead.

She took my glass and topped it off. "Grab a pillow and have a seat."

I took a drink, "Your brother has a paradise here!"

"I love coming here."

The teahouse was a 10 x 12-foot open structure with a two-foot railing connecting four corner posts that supported a hip roof of redwood shingles. The short railing kept pillows from falling into the creek. I plopped a pillow in the opposite corner and gingerly sat down. I hadn't eaten since breakfast, and the second glass went to my head.

I looked down at the water, "Are there fish in this creek?"

"Salmon run up here in the fall to spawn. Henry catches pan-size trout."

"I'm not much of an angler. What does he use for bait?"

"He uses tied flies with a bobber, but I suggest salmon eggs. There's fishing gear under the porch if you'd like to try later."

I mulled it over, "If I catch some, can we cook them up?"

"You bet. This time of year, we'll be fishing for trout. I love fresh trout and my brother taught me how to fry them in his unique way."

She relaxed with her wine and the warmth of the moment. I caught her admiring my gleaming white buttocks as I looked down at the water to spot trout.

She looked at me with a seductive grin. I knew it was time, so I looked back with raised eyebrows.

"Let's go for a swim and have sex," she said as she got up, glass and bottle in one hand.

I'd anticipated this since I got in her Hudson in San Francisco.

She dove in. I eased my way in, evaluating the water. It was cool but refreshing. Waist deep, I went under. I came up to Janet, who was waiting. She put her arms around me, planted a tongue kiss in my mouth, and reached for my butt. For the next few minutes, our bodies were entwined in sensual movement. We held onto each other well beyond our mutual orgasms, kissing and fondling.

Suddenly, Janet broke away. "Are you hungry?" she asked with a satisfied smile.

"Starving!"

She moved to the shore, dripping wet. "Let's make something to eat."

CHAPTER 4

Wet footprints dotted the wooden path and stairs leading to the upper deck. Back in the house, Janet toweled me down, caressing my head to dry my hair. Then, she dried herself while I put on shorts.

Janet pulled food out of the fridge. She wore only a T-shirt that reached her navel and no farther, leaving her bare bottom exposed.

"I have something special. Do you like Beef Stroganoff?"

"One of my favorites."

"Good. You can help."

I only thought a little about food other than eating it. But here with Janet, bare from the waist down, preparing a feast, I wondered, could this be an omen? Was this becoming a part of my life?

A London broil lay on a cutting board, bloody around the edges. Janet pointed, "You can start here. Cut this into thin eighth of an inch strips."

She handed me a knife and the wooden holder, "Make sure it's sharp!"

I tested it with my thumb, "Feels sharp."

"Let me see. It needs sharpening. Take the sharpening steel and give it a couple of swipes."

"How do you do that?"

She took the knife and swiped it back and forth over the steel. "Feel the difference?"

I felt the knife edge. The sharpened knife slid through the meat like butter.

Janet looked over, "You are a natural. Those are perfect."

She took a ten-inch skillet from under the counter and placed it on the lit burner at medium heat to melt a third of a stick of butter.

With half of the London broil cut in slices, she announced, "That's enough, Sweetie. Could you wrap the rest up in butcher paper and put it in the fridge? Hand me a couple of bowls from the upper shelf." I placed the bowls on the counter.

"Place the meat in the skillet with the melted butter. Mix it with a wooden spoon. Turn down the heat if it starts to brown."

I stirred with one hand and squeezed Janet's bare bum with the other. She held my hand on her soft flesh as she removed an onion and mushrooms from the fridge.

She turned around and kissed me on the lips. "Watch the butter!" she said as she glanced at the cooking meat. "Beautiful! Mix it up until there's no red in the meat."

She draped her arm over my shoulder, "Do you like this?"

"What part?" I answered with a sheepish grin.

"Cooking dinner with a half-naked woman."

"It would make a million men very jealous."

She kissed me again before slicing the onion and mushrooms.

"The meat looks great. Add a pinch of salt and ground pepper, then place it in the bowl. Save the butter and juices in the skillet to sauté the onions."

She took the beef from the skillet, reached down, and squeezed me. This caught me off guard, and I jumped back.

"What's the matter, Baby?" with a wink and sexy smile.

"You better be careful, Janet. This skillet is hot, and you don't have protection."

"We don't want damaged goods, do we?" she teased. "Where's the wine? We can't do this cooking without wine," she laughed.

She filled the glasses and then placed the onions into the hot skillet. We raised our glasses and took a drink. She sautéed the onions until they began to brown and then placed them in the bowl with the meat. Then, with a half stick of butter, she sautéed the mushrooms, increasing the heat slightly.

Although we'd had sex minutes earlier, watching her move around the rooms with the sexy top and bare bottom made me aroused.

"Keep an eye on those mushrooms and stir them now and again," she ordered.

She took a medium-sized pan filled with water and placed it on the burner. Her choreographed moves were entertaining to watch. She knew what came next and worked effortlessly, obviously enjoying herself.

I moved around to the other side of the counter with my wine glass, pulled out a bar stool, and sat down. Janet, standing over the skillet, looked up into my eyes. She picked up her glass, held it in salute, and winked.

She added the leftover butter to the boiling water, opened a jar of noodles, and dropped in four handfuls. She added 1/8 teaspoon of nutmeg and half a teaspoon of tarragon to the mushrooms. She briefly stirred the mix and then added one cup of sour cream to the mushrooms. White wine thinned the sour cream. Then came the meat and onions. She reduced the heat to simmer and then checked the noodles.

"Don't over cook the noodles. It's better to have them al dente, a slight bit undercooked, than overcooked and mushy," she advised.

She took out a noodle and held it with her teeth while it cooled enough to chew. When the noodles were perfect, she poured them into the colander in the sink and rinsed them with cool water to wash off the starch.

"Tony darling, bring me the plates from the table?"

She stirred the meat and sauce for the last time, then, using wooden tongs, placed a heap of noodles on the plates and spread meat sauce over them. In twenty minutes, a savory dinner was served.

I couldn't wait to dig in.

Janet took off her top and stood before me stark naked.

"Take off your shorts. Let's eat naked."

Obediently, I dropped my shorts as Janet took the plates to the dining table and returned to the kitchen for the wine. I sipped my wine while she lit the candles.

She passed me and ran her fingers through my hair. I reached up and gave her breast a gentle squeeze.

"Do you think this will do?" she asked.

"Perfect," I grinned.

By candlelight, we toasted the meal. She waited for me to have the first bite.

"This is good! So good…. Aren't you going to eat?"

"I am, I wanted to watch your reaction." she said.

The stroganoff was so good that I couldn't stop once I started. I paused long enough to have a drink of wine, and I watched Janet savor every bite.

Finished, I sat back with a glass in hand, "What's the agenda for tomorrow?"

She chewed a mouthful, swallowed, and drank before responding, "My brother and his wife will be coming sometime tomorrow. They've invited friends over tomorrow night, and we'll have a barbecue on the deck. I'm sure he'll bring steaks. I plan to make a potato salad."

She stopped long enough to take another bite of stroganoff and a sip of wine. "You've never met my brother?"

"The way you've talked about him it seems I know him."

"You don't know half of it. I told you he was married to a Russian girl, but I never told you how they met."

I shook my head, "No, you didn't," turning my chair to look directly at her.

After taking the last bite on her plate, she pushed her chair back slightly, leaned back with the glass in both hands and rested it on her tummy, the rim touching her breast.

God, this chick is sexy!

She placed her feet on my naked lap and explained her brother was the nerd of the family.

CHAPTER 5

Henry was Janet's fixer. He helped her in her quests whenever she asked. He grew up loving aviation. With a brilliant mind, he earned a scholarship to MIT. Later, he completed his postgraduate studies at Spartan College of Aeronautics and Engineering in Tulsa. Upon graduation, Grumman Aircraft Corporation courted him and brought him to their plant in Baldwin, New York, on Long Island, where they developed the Hellcat. He was working in the design and engineering department when rumblings began in Europe, and anybody with foresight could tell it wouldn't be long before Europe was at war.

When war broke out in Poland, he worked long hours at a frenzied pace. America looked on as Hitler took over Poland, France, and Belgium, and the British expeditionary forces were defeated at Dunkirk.

Before the Japanese bombed Hawaii, the U.S. established the Lend-Lease Program to aid England and Russia. Grumman played a large part in this effort, supplying aircraft parts to these countries.

With the outbreak of war, he joined the Navy to fly the Hellcat. But the Navy had other plans. They sent him to Britain and Russia to establish support networks. Heavy workloads in the States severely stifled his social life, but there was social life in England or Russia, as both countries wined and dined him to ensure his favor. That's when he met Ivana.

Ivana was a beautiful blonde with deep blue eyes. Russia assigned her to watch over him, meeting his needs. She handled every detail: transportation and translation, paid the tabs so Henry didn't cheat, and organized meals and hotel rooms. After the third night, they had sex.

Assigned as his "handler," they fell in love, which caused awkward complications. After the war, they wanted to get married and have Ivana move to the States. Going through diplomatic channels was difficult, but the Russians eventually saw the advantage of having her in America, married to a Grumman executive as the Cold War incubated.

I fondled her feet and drank my wine as Janet told the tale. I was visibly aroused.

Janet felt the hardness against the ball of her foot, "Come on, let's go take a shower and have sex. We can clean up this mess in the morning."

CHAPTER 6

An early riser, I quietly got out of bed as Janet slept. My mouth was dry, and I had a slight headache from the wine the night before. I remembered Janet telling me the fishing gear was under the deck.

The sun peeked out from the coastal mountains. I peeked at Janet through the window, peacefully sleeping. I reminisced about the 2 a.m. roust when she mounted me for a third encounter. I had unimaginable stamina.

Down the stairs, four fishing poles rigged with a small hook and buckshot weight leaned against the wall. On the table was a jar of salmon eggs. I went to the pond's edge with the eggs and a rigged pole.

I threaded three eggs on the hook and cast across the clear running stream, slowly reeling it in. In thirty seconds, a ten-inch trout was on the hook. Twenty minutes later, six trout lay in the grass when a shout came from the deck.

"Hey, Babe, what are you doing?"

"Fishing," I shouted back.

"Any luck?"

"Six in about twenty minutes."

"My word!" she giggled. "Bring them up, and we'll cook them up for breakfast."

"Be right up," turning in time to see Janet's bare bum and back.

I returned the fishing pole and salmon eggs and retrieved the fish.

Janet leaned over the sink as she finished last night's dishes. She must've gotten up soon after I did to get that accomplished.

"Those are beauties. Bring them in and put them on the counter."

She nudged her hip against mine, and we shared the tap to rinse our hands. As I dried mine, she raised her arms, dripping water off her fingertips, and hugged my neck.

She rubbed her pelvis to mine, "Did you like last night?"

"It sobered me up." I laughed.

Extending her embrace, "You ever had kedgeree?"

"What's that?"

"I'll show you. It's usually made with whitefish, but we'll use the trout instead."

"What do you want me to do?"

"Do you know how to clean fish?"

"Yes," I answered.

"Good, cut the heads off, gut them, and leave the rest whole."

The cutting board leaned against the back wall next to the stove. I took the knife I'd used the night before and sharpened it with the sharpening steel.

I placed the largest trout on the board and cut its head off. While I cut the underbelly, I asked, "Are you going to stay naked all day?"

"I'll have to put something on before my brother and his friends get here. He's more reserved than I am, you know, the odd one in the family."

We laughed together as I started at the back of the cut and cleaned out the fish guts. I ran water from the tap and cleaned out the blood along the spine.

Janet opened the rice bin, scooped out two cups, and then poured them into an eight-inch pan of boiling water. Four eggs boiled hard for ten minutes. Four spring onions were chopped and set aside. The rice boiled, the flame reduced, and the pot covered until it was fully cooked.

She placed the fish in a hot ten-inch skillet and added enough milk to cover it. Then, she added two bay leaves and turned the flame to medium heat.

"These simmer in the milk." she said.

I never realized cooking could be so much fun and rewarding. I stood beside Janet, watching the milk boil over the fresh trout.

"The fun part is when the trout has cooked." she said.

She turned off the flame and placed the cutting board beside the skillet.

"Now watch this," as she gingerly lifted the skin off the fish. She pinched the backbone at the front and pulled the spine and ribs out in one piece.

"See how easy that was?" she asked.

"Looks pretty easy."

"Give it a try. When you get the bones out, mash up the fish into small pieces."

I finished boning the trout and mashed them on a plate. "What do you want me to do with these?"

"Add them to the mix. Add the pan of rice to the skillet with the mashed eggs.... Oh wait, do me a favor, Sweetie, and look in the pantry for a small can of peas. The opener is in the drawer."

She drained the can of peas and stirred them into the mixture, adding salt and pepper.

"Get the curry powder from the spice rack. I'm going to need about a teaspoonful," she ordered.

Janet stirred in the mashed trout with the curry and declared, "I think we have it!"

She turned off the flame, "Yogurt will finish it up."

Over her shoulder, she asked, "Can you open a bottle of champagne and bring orange juice from the fridge? I'm sure there is one in the wine rack."

"Is Brut all right?"

"That will be fine."

She placed a healthy portion of kedgeree on each plate.

I took orange juice out of the fridge and couldn't resist pressing the cold bottle against her bare bum as she passed.

"Ouch!" she shouted, "That's cold; you're so mean!"

We laughed and entered the dining room.

Champagne and orange juice were on the table. I went to the glass-fronted cabinet full of elegant crystal and removed two wine glasses.

She brought the yogurt, "Ice. We need ice for the mimosas!" She returned to the ice box, taking the glasses with her.

I tackled the bottle of champagne, gently untwisted the wire holding in the cork, and carefully worked it out of the bottle until there was a loud pop. It flew to the ceiling with no bubbly gushing out. Janet placed three ice cubes in each glass. I half-filled them, leaving room to top them off with orange juice. Janet stirred them with her index finger.

Our glasses touched. Savoring the drinks, "Great morning drink," I commented.

"Isn't it?" she smiled. "You haven't had kedgeree before?"

"No, where is it from?"

"Scotland. It's an old Scottish fisherman's meal made with haddock or other white fish, but since you caught trout, I thought we'd try trout kedgeree. Here's what you do," she continued, "Take a spoonful of the yogurt and put it on top or on the side of your plate."

She placed yogurt on top of the kedgeree and took a bite.

"Not bad," she proclaimed, "In fact, pretty damn good!"

She watched me do the same, "What do you think?"

"Delicate….it has a delicate taste."

"Perfect! Yes, it does."

After our meal, I asked, "How will your brother feel about you hanging out with a younger guy?"

"Are you getting nervous?"

"I want to be cool, but feel I'll be a little out of place. I'm going to feel awkward."

"Don't worry. My brother understands me. Just be yourself."

"That's the problem, I'm not sure who I am around people like your brother."

"Here's what we do, we'll get dressed to start with."

"I wondered about that," I laughed.

"Henry likes to dress properly for evenings."

"That's why you had me bring my dress shirt and tie?"

"Exactly, I thought you'd be more comfortable dressed up around him and his friends. How are you at mixing drinks?"

"What kind of drinks?"

"Martinis, bloody mary's, gin and tonic, margaritas, things like that."

"Do you expect me to be the bartender?"

"People like my brother appreciate people who can mix a mean martini."

"I see where this is going. You're trying to bring me up."

"Everybody must start somewhere. To the posh, it helps to have certain social skills."

"I never considered myself posh. Do you consider yourself posh?"

"I've been called that, among other things," she laughed.

"Isn't that lifestyle some sort of game?"

"You can call it that, and I'd say, yes, but with our station in life, it's what's expected."

"Our station in life?" I questioned.

"Yes, Tony, our station in life. Sweetheart, we're rich and free. The world is out there for the taking. It's all a game."

Smiling, I asked, "How do you make a mean martini?"

"Come on, I'll show you how."

Janet took my arm and led me to the kitchen, "Now watch me."

She took fresh lemon, green olives, and cocktail picks from the cupboard, then threaded two olives on each pick and cut the lemon slices in half.

"Look in the liquor cabinet and bring some gin."

Gordon's London Dry Gin was in the front of the cabinet.

"Pour two ounces of gin into the shaker with a quarter ounce of vermouth, add a couple of ice cubes, and shake. Strain the alcohol into the glass, twist the lemon, add the olives."

She handed me the drink, "Try this and tell me what you think."

It cleared the other tastes from breakfast, "Great!"

Janet looked up at the clock, "Shit! My brother will be here in an hour. We've got to clean this place up!"

Shocked back to reality from this alcoholic fog, "What do you want me to do?"

"Clear off the table. I'll run the hot water and start cleaning the kitchen."

The place was cleaned within the hour, and we went upstairs.

"Put on your dress pants, dress shirt with tie and a pullover sweater," she instructed.

She wore a sheer black dress that exposed her cleavage and shapely body, paired with simple black pumps. Her hair was jumbled, but sexy looking.

While checking the martini supplies in the liquor cabinet, I heard her say, "Grab a beer out of the fridge and bring me one. Let's sit here a bit and relax before they arrive."

Too far gone to refuse, I handed Janet a beer.

Janet took a couple of drinks from her bottle and looked up. "You look good, cleaned up and with clothes on. I think you'll do fine," she said.

I chuckled and wondered if this was a game I wanted to play. I let out a big sigh. I was one of the players.

"You know, Janet, you're goddamn sexy yourself. I'm looking forward to meeting your brother."

CHAPTER 7

oving day finally came. I drove over the Golden Gate Bridge with my meager belongings and thought about the night spent with Janet's brother and friends at the cabin. I had held up my end and received rave reviews for the martinis.

I pulled into the marina parking lot at 10:30 a.m. Carl and Megan had to catch a plane at 2 p.m. for La Paz, Mexico, and from there, take a bus down to the small fishing village of Cabo San Lucas, where they had rented a house for six months.

Carl was commissioned to produce a book on organic gardening. He was taking down boxes filled with research materials to use in his book.

Megan was an artist. The nude painting hanging in their living room was a self-portrait from Carl's photographs. She looked to the Mexican locals for her subjects. She had boxes filled with art materials.

I was excited to begin my new adventure as I approached the boathouse. As I got closer, I heard Carl and Megan banging and yelling as they finished packing for their adventure. "Fuck you," I heard Carl yell. "Get your ass over here and help me pack, Megan. Or I can leave you here. Either way works for me."

Not wanting to interrupt the yelling, I banged on the door.

Megan scurried past the open front door with an armful of stuff, glanced up, and saw me standing outside.

"Tony!" she blurted out. "You wouldn't believe it; we had this stuff packed up when asshole Carl decided to go through it again to make sure he had everything. For Christ's sake, he had months to do this. I'm madder than hell. Our friends are going to be here in less than an hour to take us to the airport, and we must go through this again!"

From the backroom, Carl yelled, "Shut the fuck up, Megan, and get on with it. If you'd quit bitching, we'll get this finished in time."

Megan turned and ran back inside.

I followed her into the bedroom. "What can I do to help?"

"Thank you," Megan responded. "Could you carry these sealed boxes and load them into our van? Thank you, Sweetie. That would be an immense help!"

I carried boxes to the parking lot, glad to be away from the heavy vibes from the houseboat.

As Carl predicted, getting everything in order didn't take long. After I'd made a couple of trips to the van, the situation quieted down. I felt uncomfortable and realized they were giving each other the silent treatment. It's not a terrific way to start a six-month excursion to Mexico.

Their friends showed up on time and helped with the last details. Inside Carl's van, and with hugs and kisses, they were off. Glad it was over. I brought in my stuff to get organized. It was hard to grasp that I now lived on a houseboat in Sausalito, California. As I sat out on the deck enjoying my new surroundings, a flock of ducks swam by, looking for a handout.

Janet planned to come over to welcome me aboard and make sure I had food on hand. But for the moment, I was glad to be by myself to get the feel of the place.

It didn't take long before curious neighbors showed up to investigate the new person on the docks. The first was a short, thin, older gentleman in his late seventies. My attention turned from the ducks to the funny-looking old guy watching my every move.

An old white captain's hat framed his tanned, weather-beaten face. Around his neck was a multi-colored thin scarf tucked into the collar of a red and white striped dress shirt. He wore a blue blazer over the shirt, white trousers, and blue canvas deck shoes. A Yorkshire Terrier, wearing a pink bow and a purple sweater, had a leash attached to its collar. The old man had wrapped it around his wrist.

We stared at each other. Finally, the old man spoke. "Hello. My name is Jack Daniels, but they call me Whiskey."

I jumped to my feet to shake his hand. "Hi, I'm Tony Taylor. Nice to meet you."

"We've been waiting for your arrival. Carl told us they were going to have someone stay here while they were away."

"Brian helped me find this place. It's a dream come true for me."

"We know that too," reaching down to pick up his dog. "Brian is one of our favorites. If he recommended you, I'm sure you'll fit in."

I wondered when he meant to *fit in.*

Glancing at his dog, "This is Billy," he said. "He's my pride and joy. He's getting a bit on nowadays, but the best friend I ever had." He lifted Billy up to his cheek and gently squeezed him.

I wasn't a dog person, but I made eye contact with Billy and smiled at him. I waited to hear what Whiskey had to say next.

The old man blurted out, "Oh God! Here comes Maud. I knew she'd be one of the first to come down here."

A plump woman in her mid to late fifties shuffled in our direction. She wore flannel pajamas underneath an open, loose-fitting silk robe frayed at the edges. Her feet were covered in worn-out bedroom slippers. She had curlers in her hair and bright red lipstick smeared over her lips. A half-burned-out cigarette hung between her fingers in her left hand, and in her right was a tall, sweaty glass of bloody mary. She shuffled in our direction.

She yelled in a crackled voice, "I saw you standing down here, Whiskey, and I come to see what you were up to. It looks to me like you're meeting our new neighbor."

"That's right," Whiskey returned. "I knew you wouldn't be able to stay away for long. This is Tony," looking back at me. "What did you say your last name was again?"

"Taylor."

"Tony Taylor." Whiskey shouted out.

"Hello, Tony Taylor!"

She put the half-burned cigarette to her lips and changed hands with her bloody mary. "I'm Maud."

Cold and wet from her drink, her right hand took my hand, cigarette ash falling to the deck.

"Awful nice to meet you."

"Nice to meet you, too."

I tried to figure out how to get back to the solitude of watching my ducks from the parade of people showing up when a guy came from the opposite direction. As he passed, I noticed his black leather trousers had the backside cut out, exposing both cheeks of his ass. He wore a leather vest over a bare snow-white hairless chest and a live cockatoo perched on his shoulder. On his feet were black leather biker boots, his head covered with a red bandana. To top it off, gold chains of assorted sizes hung from his neck.

The man wasn't interested in what was happening, but wanted to join the group. Neither Maud nor Whiskey acknowledged his presence, but continued their conversation about how Carl and Megan were now gone, how I had taken their place, and how they were going to adjust to the change.

It was a weird scenario for me to get used to. I was ready to run, but just then, Janet came down the dock to the rescue.

Janet could tell by my fidgeting that I was uncomfortable. She put her hand on my shoulder as if to steady me and keep me from taking off. "Are you settled in now? Do you have enough food?"

I welcomed the familiar face. "Not really. I need to go shopping."

Janet visited Brian at the marina. The locals knew her well, and she acknowledged their presence as old friends. They lit up as she approached.

"All right, give Tony space so he can settle in his new place. We must go shopping."

Whiskey responded, "OK, Janet. You take care of Tony. We wanted him to know he was welcome. We'll have time to get to know him."

Leatherman didn't say anything. He turned and walked away with his bare buns exposed and the cockatoo looking back from his shoulder.

"Let's go check out the kitchen. Odd people live on these houseboats, that's what makes it so much fun. You'll find they're good-hearted, once you understand their costumes," she laughed.

"I found it strange. I'm glad you came when you did. The guy who cut out the buns of his leather pants was weird."

Janet began to laugh, unable to control her laughter. "That's Harold. He's about the weirdest, but harmless. He never says much, but always seems to be around. These people accepted him for who he is. I find him entertaining."

We entered the kitchen and found a note left by Megan on the counter.

Tony, feel free to use up anything here you want. There is meat in the freezer. Sorry about the vegetables; they are getting old. Check things out. It's all yours.

"That makes it easy," said Janet as she looked around. "They don't have much here. Even the spice rack is bare."

She went through the kitchen, opening and closing cabinet doors.

"I'll tell you what. Let's throw out what you won't use and restock. They must not eat at home much."

She tossed old food and other unnecessary items in paper bags to haul to the trash.

"With Brian around you'll never go hungry. He brings food home, plus practices new recipes in his kitchen. You took to cooking at the cabin. I can tell you have talent. This might be a new beginning for you, plus Brian loves to show off his new work, and he'll need a taster. You might be it."

Taster? I wondered what kind of taster she had in mind. Megan had told me Brian was gay, and that made me very uncomfortable. I carried the bags to the trash, thinking Janet had something up her sleeve when she told me cooking might be a new beginning for me. I enjoyed the culinary aspects of life and wanted to learn more.

Back at the houseboat, Janet finished in the kitchen. I could now call the place mine.

"I'm starving. Come on, I'll take you out to dinner at The Seahorse."

I was hungry and didn't want to mess up the place, "OK, let's go."

"Let's walk. It's a bit of a hike, but you'll see the waterfront. Their seafood is great, with a view of the bay. We should celebrate!"

She rushed off. When I locked the door, I had to hurry to catch up as I carried the last of the trash bags. "Wait up. You must be hungry!"

We walked down Bridgeway Avenue. I needed to confess to Janet how I felt about Brian's sexual orientation, but I didn't know how to put it into words.

Finally, I blurted, "Janet, there's something I have to talk to you about."

The way I said it caught her off guard. She stopped and looked at me, confused, "Am I doing something wrong?"

"No, it's not you."

She released her breath, "Thank God, the way you said it scared me."

"Sorry, but I don't know how to bring up what I want to say."

"Can't you just say it? It can't be that weird."

I hesitated, "It's not weird, it's that...."

"Come on Tony, you know you can tell me anything. What is it?"

"Megan told me Brian was a homosexual and I'm uncomfortable around that type of person."

Janet looked up, "Oh that," and began to laugh.

Confused by her response, I lost control of myself, "What's so funny, I don't know Brian that well and I don't want a come-on where I feel intimidated. He helped me out and I don't know what his expectations might be. I'm not a queer and don't plan to become one. How do I deal with this?"

Janet was quiet for a while. "Brian is a sensitive guy. If something gets weird, talk to him about it. If you are up front with your fears, he'll respect that. I know Brian. Besides, he'd have to fight me for you. He and I are friends, and sometimes a bit more. Anyway, he knows you're mine and he will respect that."

"Thanks, Janet. I feel better. I'm looking forward to The Seahorse and a great dinner."

CHAPTER 8

The Seahorse is a quaint restaurant with outside tables overlooking the marinas. When we entered, the dinner crowd was already arriving.

The host was a man in his fifties. He wore black trousers, a starched white shirt, and a black bow tie. When Janet requested seating on the patio, he motioned toward the open space overlooking the water and said, "Take any table you like."

We took a table next to the railing while the host handed us menus and took our drink order of house red as we enjoyed the view facing the bay.

The drinks arrived along with a basket of sourdough with garlic butter, "The waitress will be here shortly to take your order."

I sipped the wine, reached over, took a piece of bread, and studied the menu.

"What do you suggest?" I asked.

"I'm going to have halibut steak. But it is all good."

"That sounds good, but I'm going to have seafood pasta. I love scallops, shrimp, and mussels. Oh, and octopus. I've never had octopus."

We closed our menus. The server returned with more bread and took our orders.

While we waited for our food, Janet was fiddling with her napkin. I could tell she was nervous.

"Now it's your turn," I said. "Do you have something to say and don't know how to say it?"

She looked at me with a nervous smile, tapping her fingernails on the table.

"I want to let you in on a secret."

"What kind of a secret?" I laughed.

"Brian and I have been friends for a long time."

"Yes," as I squirmed in my seat. "Does this secret have anything to do with me?"

"It could."

She buttered a piece of bread and took a bite, followed by a sip of wine.

I put both hands behind my head and looked directly at her. "What do you mean it could?"

She took another bite, and her eyes seemed to focus on the glass as she toyed with it in her hands. "I'll start from the beginning."

I leaned back into the chair. "I hope this isn't a weird cult, Janet. I'm not into things like that. I'm an independent guy."

"I know, I know. Don't rush to conclusions before I explain. This could be something you might enjoy. It's fun, and you'll travel and meet very interesting people."

"Interesting people? You mean like the ones at the marina?" I leaned forward to drink wine, "All right, tell me about this secret."

"Brian and I belong to a secret worldwide culinary society. It's a game really. The object is to try and steal recipes from other people in the society and gain an advantage over them."

"That's it?"

"That's it."

"What's the big deal? Why the secrecy? Sounds a bit lame to me."

"The big deal is, people in this society take it very seriously, and we spend money doing it. The competition is fierce with no holds barred."

The server brought the food and asked if we wanted another glass of wine.

"We would," said Janet without giving me a choice.

I wondered if what Janet was saying was real. Do people really do this kind of thing?

"Here," said Janet, "I'll show you what I mean. Take a bite of your seafood pasta."

I rolled pasta onto the fork and took a bite.

"Now try some of the seafood."

I cut a piece of octopus and put it in my mouth. It was moist and chewy.

"Do you like it?"

Still chewing, "Yes, fantastic!"

"Do you know why?"

"Not really," I answered, looking confused.

"I'll tell you why. The chef back in the kitchen knows what to add and how to prepare it to give your taste buds an orgasm. It's his special recipe he developed for your pleasure."

Janet cut a piece of her halibut and took a bite.

"Umm, splendid," she remarked. "You see, this is how the chef makes his mark. He has something special that's his, and he won't give his secrets to anybody. It's his life."

She paused for a moment so we could enjoy the meal. "Let me give you an example. You like French fries, don't you?"

"Sure, I do."

"What makes them taste so good?"

"Oh hell, I don't know."

"It's the salt. Would you want French fries without salt?"

"I suppose not."

"How do you think that octopus would taste without anything added to it?"

"I'm not sure. This is the first time I ate one."

"He knows what to add to bring the best flavor. That's his secret. He wants to bring you back repeatedly. He wants you to tell your friends, so they enjoy what you're enjoying now. That gives him pleasure, and he makes money."

She took another bite of halibut and washed it down with wine. "What I am talking about is a group of people who want to give you a culinary orgasm, and they don't want others to know how they did it. It's their special little secret. What we do is break their code and gain an advantage over them. It's a fun game, with great food. We add adventure to our culinary experience."

I struggled to understand what she was saying. Where did I fit into their scheme?

I realized that Janet's suggestion that the chef adds things to bring out these flavors was true. I'd never considered this before, and as this was my first culinary orgasm, I wanted to know more.

I looked at Janet. "Where do I fit in this plan? I get the game, but what exactly is the plan?"

"It's too early to say. Besides, I think it'd be best for you to get to know Brian and think about it." She took her last bite. "God, was that good! He really knows how to bring out the best in a piece of halibut."

After we finished our meal, we sat quietly for a moment and took the last drink of wine. Then, the server reappeared and asked if we'd like dessert.

I glanced at her and said, "Not for me, thanks. I'm stuffed, but give my compliments to the chef."

"I will. Marcus will appreciate that," the server answered.

"None for me either, but I'll take the check."

Janet reached into her purse and took out cash, including a healthy tip.

"Come on, let's go. We can stop by Paul's Grocery Store on the way back and pick up things to hold you over until we can do real shopping."

CHAPTER 9

At Paul's, we bought items to keep me going, along with mid-priced wines. Back at the houseboat, Janet opened a bottle. I was still feeling the effects of the restaurant wine and trying to understand the secret culinary society Janet had thrown at me during lunch. She went out on the deck, moving a chair near the railing to put her feet up. She lifted her skirt to get the sun on her legs.

"This is going to be great, just great," she shouted toward the house.

I moved a chair next to hers, took my glass, settled into the chair, and put my feet next to hers.

She looked over the bay, "I must go to New York for a couple of days to meet with clients."

"New York! That's a long way. You are kind of my safety net."

She patted my arm. "I know, but a big art show is coming, and they want to put pieces on the market."

"What kind of pieces?"

"Rembrandts. They're owned by a Jewish family in New York. They want to bring over family members who survived the Nazi prison camps. If they get a decent price for the paintings, it could get them settled with a start in business."

"How much do you think you can get for them?"

"I'm not sure. I'll do the appraisal, thinking I can get a million and a half for both. That'd be a nice nest egg, don't you think?"

"It sure would, plus a nice commission for you."

"About 10%. That's what I do," she said, finishing her wine.

She got up from her chair. "I'd love to spend the night with you in your new place, but I've got to get ready for my trip. Bring the bottle in with you and we'll have a quickie to see how the mattress works."

I hesitated momentarily as she approached the door, stopped, and looked back. "You are coming?"

CHAPTER 10

The following day, the sun came through the bedroom window. I rolled over on my stomach to see Richardson Bay and Harbor Point. It was a beautiful morning, not a wisp of wind on the water. A wooden sailboat motored by for a day sail on San Francisco Bay. The scent of Janet's perfume was on the pillow.

Barefoot, I went out on the deck to breathe fresh air. It was so new, I couldn't believe it was real. Raising my arms to stretch, I turned and saw Brian sitting on his deck reading the local paper, a cup of coffee in his hand.

"Good morning," he called out. "I have fresh coffee and sweet rolls. Come on down."

I remembered Brian's last cup of coffee, so I didn't hesitate to approach his deck.

"Have a seat," placing the coffee and rolls before me.

"How was your first night?"

"Very nice," I said as I reached for a roll.

Brian folded the paper, laid it on the bench next to the railing, and leaned back in his chair.

"These sweet rolls are good! Did you make them?"

He laughed, "No. I get them from the bakery at the hotel I'm working for right now. Pretty good, aye?" taking one for himself.

"Did you just get up?" I asked.

"Me? No, I haven't gone to bed yet. I put on a big dinner for a women's charity group last night, I didn't get home until 4:30. When I do that type of event, prima donnas need a lot of attention. I get hyped, and it takes me a while to settle down."

"Do you do that kind of event a lot?"

"I don't like doing big events. A friend of mine put it on and used my name to draw in more people. The money is good. By the way, Janet is off to New York today."

"She's doing art appraisals. She helped me get into Carl and Megan's place, and we went to dinner."

"Where'd she take you?"

"The Seahorse. It was really good." I remembered the secret society. Should I mention it? I decided to wait.

"Marcus, the chef there, I've known for years. He puts together fine dishes."

I decided to ask him about being gay. I could feel my face burning. "I've heard some interesting things about you."

"You mean my homosexuality?"

Caught off guard, my face turned from hot to on fire. "We might as well get the subject out front. I think you're a cool guy, but I want you to know, I'm not attracted to men sexually and plan to stay that way."

"Are you sure?"

"Yes, I'm sure. How does a hetero guy have a friendship with a homo guy and not always have to look back and think he's trying to fuck him in the ass?"

Brian laughed and put his cup on the table. "You can never be too sure."

I squinted eye to eye-with Brian. I missed the humor in his remark.

Brian looked straight at me, "If I can't have you, I can still make a play for Harold and his cockatoo. He's well worn, but any port in a storm."

I realized Brian was joking, and as the absurdity hit me, I burst out laughing with Brian.

"Besides, Janet doesn't like to share her toys. So, you're safe there. I've got enough problems to deal with, and I don't need any more."

Brian got up to get more coffee, "Want another cup?"

"I don't want to hold you up."

He shouted from inside, "You're not holding me up. I'm taking the next couple of days off."

I was relieved to air the issue and glad he was good-natured about it. I figured he'd been through this scenario before without denting his self-confidence.

He brought out the coffee and changed the subject. "Now that you're moved into your new place, what's on your agenda?"

"My mother's coming today to see the place, and we're going out to lunch. She's curious and wants to see where I live."

"That'll be nice. Where are you taking her?"

"The only place I know is The Seahorse. I'll take her there."

"I'm sure she'll like it. Think she'll like your new digs?"

"I don't know. She likes Sausalito. She comes here often with her girlfriends. I doubt she imagined I'd be living here on a houseboat. What are your plans?"

"I have an idea for a seafood dish. I'm heading to the seafood market."

"Do you mind me asking what you're going to try?"

"Not at all. In fact, if you're around later you can come over and see what I'm doing and be the first to have a taste."

Curiosity got the best of me. "What will it be?"

"I have this idea to wrap an oyster in a thin layer of salmon and lightly bake it."

"I like salmon and oysters, but never thought about the two together."

"Me neither," he said. "I might add a sprinkle of fresh ginger over the top, to give it a little bite."

"Sounds great!" I said and looked at my watch. "I better get going; I've got some cleaning up to do before my mom comes."

"You better. I know how moms are, and we don't want to give her a bad impression," Brian laughed.

He stood up and stuck out his hand. I shook it heartily.

"Thanks for the coffee and rolls."

"No problem. You're going to fit in fine."

Back at the houseboat, I thought about what Janet said. She was right. Brian was a cool guy, plus I looked forward to oysters wrapped in salmon. The idea of the secret society and where I fit in was still on my mind. I'd ask him about it when we met later.

CHAPTER 11

Mom arrived at the marina in her new Lincoln at the wrong time. Dressed fashionably—not typical for the marina—she exited her car. The first thing she saw was Harold, cockatoo on his shoulder, wearing ventilated leather pants. He stared at her.

She was nervous as he watched her walk her down the dock.

She scanned the dock for the slip number. As she passed the other boats, she came upon Whiskey, holding his dog while he talked with Maud.

Maud, in her night clothes, bloody mary in her right hand, cigarette in her left, smeared lipstick around her lips, greeted her, saying, "Good morning."

She nodded and hurried down the dock.

When she arrived at my houseboat, she seemed shocked. I was straightening up, looking forward to showing her the coolness of my new digs, when I heard her call out, "TONY!"

I rushed out to greet her, but there was no smile on her lips, only fire in her eyes.

"Hi Mom, come aboard."

She stood motionless. "What in the hell goes on around here?"

"What do you mean?" I innocently responded.

"Who are these crazy people I passed?"

"Who are you talking about?"

"I'm talking about this crazy guy with his butt exposed and some weirdo in a captain's hat next to a sloppy old lady drinking a bloody mary in her night clothes."

"Oh them; they live here."

"I figured that. How did you find this place? If your father knew you lived in a place like this, he'd be very disappointed!"

"Oh Mom, calm down. Please, come aboard. It's not what you think."

I rushed to the dock to help her down the gangway. She hesitated until I took her hand and tugged a little to get her moving. She resisted at first, but then I coaxed her aboard.

She was still on the deck of the houseboat when I prodded, "Don't you think this is nice Mom?"

Not saying anything, she stood and looked around.

"Please come in."

I took her hand and led her inside, where she stood frowning. After her eyes adjusted to the bright sunlight, they darted around the room, focusing on the painting of the nude woman.

"Who is that?!" she demanded, staring at the picture.

I was determined to distract her. I pulled her toward the kitchen.

"Here, look at this nice kitchen. Look at the bedroom."

Slowly, she let me pull her in my direction, still speechless. She inspected the bedroom with the small bath and shower, then returned to the kitchen. She leaned against the counter and placed her handbag on the redwood countertop. She folded her arms on her chest and continued to look around.

I waited for her to say something. Finally, she puckered her lips and raised her eyebrows. "It does have its charm."

I broke out in a smile, "It does, doesn't it, Mom!"

"I suppose."

She pivoted and turned on the faucet, feeling the water through her fingers.

"Mom, where do you want to go for lunch?"

"I know a place, but you pick."

"How about The Seahorse?"

By the time we got to The Seahorse, she had calmed down and was in an improved mood. We sat at the same table Janet and I had the day before.

The waiter brought the menus.

She looked at the menu. "Speaking of horses, I went to the stables to check on your horse, Pickle. It looked like she was missing you."

"I've been meaning to get out and take her for a run, but with moving, I haven't had a chance."

"You ride like the wind. I'm wondering if you've lost interest in riding now that you're grown up. I know things change as we get older."

"To be honest, I have lost interest. What do you think we should do?"

"What are your plans?"

"I met people in the culinary world. They're really dedicated to their art, and I'm looking forward to learning more from them."

"That's something new. What brought that on?"

"I watched them put together different ingredients to catch the right taste. It's scientific."

"Scientific? Sounds like you're taken by it. I wonder what your father would say about his son being a chef?"

"I'm not saying I'm going to be a chef, Mom. I never thought about the culinary side of things. And the more I learn, I wouldn't mind knowing more about it, if for no other reason than being able to put together tasty dishes."

"You dabble in it, and when you produce something tasty, you bring it home for me and your father. I'm sure he'd appreciate it. You know I would."

"That's a deal, Mom. You can count on it. I can't think of anything I'd rather do."

After a wonderful lunch, we returned to the marina and said our goodbyes with a hug and a kiss. "Sweetheart, do your mom a favor and go check in on Pickle. Please figure out what you want to do with her."

"I will Mom."

Mother's approval, partial though it was, put my mind at ease. My livelihood depended on the allowance I received. It was the only way I could afford this space and the opportunity to investigate the culinary society and its secrets.

CHAPTER 12

That evening, after Mom left, Brian called from the dock. "Tony, you in there?"

I stuck my head out. "What's up?"

"I got the ingredients. Come on down when you get a minute, and I'll show you something."

I didn't want to seem too anxious, "I'll be down in a bit, I need to do a few things first."

"I'm going to start right away. Don't want you to miss anything."

"Be there in a flash."

It was time to ask questions about the Culinary Society. What was Brian's role? Did he know what Janet had planned for me? I knew decision time was coming, and I wanted answers to my questions. Just like my worries about Brian, I wanted to make sure I knew what was in the future for me. *Surprise* was a dirty word!

I waited a full five minutes before going to Brian's boat. I walked down the gangway; the door was open, and I stuck my head in.

The interior was a big kitchen with a large cutting-board table in the middle. A small pile of oysters was on one end of the cutting board. A large oven with a gas grill nestled between the countertops on the back wall. Dishes and plates of every size and shape were in the cabinets. Cooking utensils, iron skillets, pots, and pans hung from the ceiling within an arm's length from any part of the room.

Brian leaned over a sizable, deep porcelain sink while he washed down a ten-pound salmon.

"Come on in, I'm just getting started," and placed the dripping salmon on the newspaper next to the oysters.

"What do you think of my laboratory?"

"What do you call it?" I laughed.

"It might be hard to imagine, but when I'm here, I'm trying out new stuff. I love what I do."

"It looks like you have everything down to a fine science."

"You think so? Let's start."

Brian reached for a filet knife. He assessed the edge with his thumb for sharpness, then took the sharpening steel. "One of the secrets is to have very sharp knives." He ran the edge over the steel.

"At Janet's cabin we made Beef Stroganoff. She had me cut the meat, but not before a sharpening lesson."

"Ah good. She's started to break you in. I've been up there, a beautiful place."

"It is. Very private."

"Don't suppose she was wearing any clothes?"

"Not a stitch," I laughed.

"Enough said," he picked up a towel to dry his hands. "Let's have a glass of wine. It's always better to have a glass of wine when you try out new things. I can't do this at work." He turned to a small wine rack on the wall next to the bedroom door, "What do you prefer?"

"Doesn't matter to me."

"Let's try the claret." He reached for the opener hanging from a hook under the rack. "This claret is from France and is cheaper than the California wines. It always amazes me how they can do it. It's an exceptionally fine wine."

Brian opened the bottle and poured two glasses of wine. "Try it. Tell me what you think."

He swished the wine in his glass, assessed the aroma, and sipped for flavor.

Watching Brian, I lifted the glass to my lips for a taste, "It's pretty good—sharper than the Merlot Janet likes, but good."

"You noticed! You have the makings of a wine connoisseur."

Brian looked at the salmon on the cutting board. "This salmon is whole. That's how I buy it, as fresh as possible, right off the boat, with the slime left on the outside."

"You think you would want it gutted and cleaned first."

"That's what most people think. But to have fresh fish you need guts and everything. That way it holds in its flavor longer. The minute you cut it open it starts to rot."

He cut along the top right next to the dorsal fin. The knife was so sharp he hardly applied any pressure as he made a small cut from the gill to the tail.

He brought his knife back up to the head behind the gill, cutting top down, around the pectoral fin.

"I try not to cut into the sack that holds the guts."

I watched Brian and learned that retaining natural flavors is a special art. There was much to learn about what made Brian unique in his craft.

He placed a thumb in the uppercut and sliced the skin and meat from the backbone. He cut through the pin bones with three slices of the knife, and a perfect filet lay on the cutting board with the guts still in place. He turned over the salmon and repeated the procedure. In seconds, two perfectly cut filets lay together.

The rest of the carcass lay on the newspaper. He rolled it up in the paper and handed it to me, saying, "Here, throw this mess into the bay."

"What about the paper?" I asked.

"Throw it in. The paper will dissolve and go out with the tide."

He took a shucking knife and a pair of needle-nosed pliers from a drawer next to the oven and placed them on the cutting board.

"Now you can help me. First wash your hands and grab a towel."

Gently feeling down the middle of the filet, "You can feel these small pin bones sticking out."

I traced my finger along the filet, feeling the pin bones.

With the pliers, Brian took hold of the end of the bone and pulled it out. "You do this while I shuck the oysters." He handed me the pliers.

Brian angled the shucking knife in a small indentation at the hinge of the oyster shell. With pressure and a twist, the oyster popped open. He scraped the fresh oyster from the shell into the white ceramic bowl. The shells landed in the bucket on the floor.

He reached for the next oyster, "Ever since Roman times, oysters have been considered an aphrodisiac."

"What does it do for you?" I asked.

"They give more stamina in love making."

"How do they know that?"

"They tried it with and without oysters and found better results with the oysters."

I kept that in mind and pulled out the pin bones until a small pile of bones lay on the cutting board while Brian finished shucking the oysters.

"What do you want me to do with these bones?"

"Are you sure you got them all?" he checked the filets. "Here, you missed two."

"I did?" and checked again. "Oh yeah, I did." Pulling the last two, I felt a bit embarrassed.

"Have you ever missed any?"

"Not usually, the last thing you want is to serve a bone in a seafood meal. That could get you in trouble if it ever got caught in your customer's throat."

I took my towel off my shoulder and cleaned my hands. Brian took another drink and reached under the table, picking up the bucket with the shells, "Put your fish bones in here."

I set the bucket on the floor, wiped my hands, then finished my claret.

He set the oven at 350 degrees to preheat, took out a metal baking tray, and placed it on the table. After spreading olive oil onto the metal tray, he washed it off his fingers, dried them, and freshened my glass.

I pulled a stool out from under the table and sat, resting my glass on the corner of the table. "This is interesting. What do we do next?"

"What I'm attempting to do is cut paper thin slices of salmon from the top of these filets, thin enough you can almost see through them."

He chose a wider knife, sharpened it, and took a drink. He carefully studied the filets.

I leaned forward and focused on what Brian was about to do.

He started his cut and looked up, "See how this filet is a mounded? I will shave a little off the top to get a flat surface. I want to get down to where each slice is about three inches wide."

"That's going to be tricky," I noted, engrossed in the process.

He reached for his glass and took a drink, "We have two filets, so the first one might be practice."

He used the word "WE." This word made me feel included in the experiment without being responsible for the outcome.

"I'll cut a section off the tail and practice."

He cut a four-inch section off the main filet and flattened the knife. He cut an eighth-inch thick slice of salmon with an even, continuous movement. Then, he held the slice to the light coming from the window. The middle was dark, but light came through on the edges.

"This is going to work," he said as he made another uniform cut.

When he held it up, light shone through the entire filet. He perfected the process and repeated it with the full filet.

"That will do it," he said, holding the last slice to the light.

I looked at the translucent salmon, "You're an artist!"

He cut two equal pieces, three inches wide and five inches long, and placed them on the oiled metal tray.

"Before I cut any more, I'm going to see how I can wrap these around an oyster."

He placed an oyster on top of the slice of salmon, lifted the corners like a basket, delicately rolled it over, and tucked the sides underneath the oyster.

"What do you think, Tony? I'll go for eight pieces, which will give us four apiece."

"Sounds good to me, can't wait to try them."

He gathered the waste, placed it in the bucket, and handed it to me.

"You know where this goes?"

"In the bay."

"Exactly."

I took the bucket out on the deck. I thought the ducks might enjoy the salmon waste, so I tossed it to them. They went for it with a vengeance, fighting each other for the most significant piece. More ducks flew in, quacking loudly, demanding their share. This created quite a duck ruckus, which attracted the local seagulls, who entered the fray and dived through the ducks.

The birds became so noisy that Brian stuck his head out the door. "What in the hell is going on out there?"

"The birds showed up."

"I guess so," he laughed. "You better get your ass back in here before they shit all over you."

I covered my head with my free arm and retreated inside.

The first bottle of claret was empty, so Brian asked, "Could you get another bottle and open it?"

I opened the second bottle and freshened the glasses while Brian grated and sprinkled fresh ginger on the salmon.

He looked at his work, "I'll add dried celery. Do you know that if you eat three stalks of celery and then pass by a woman, she'll want to kiss you?"

Fascinated, "Really?" I answered, feeling the wine going to my head.

"Proven fact. I challenge you to try it."

He set down the jar of dried celery, wiped his hands, and picked up the tray of salmon oyster mounds.

"How do you know this?" I asked.

He slid the tray into the oven, "Because I'm a chef," taking another drink.

Brian and Janet had hidden knowledge I wanted in on. I wanted to know the secrets hidden in diverse types of food. No longer concerned, through this alcoholic fog, this secret culinary society was for me.

"Janet told me about this secret culinary society. She told me you two were in on it and want me to get involved,"

"How much did she tell you?"

"It's a worldwide group, which could be fun where I'd meet interesting people and travel the world eating great food."

"That's what she said, did she?" He opened the oven door to check on the salmon mounds. He reached for a fork and gently touched the mounds to check for firmness.

"It's a little more than that," he said, setting down the fork and taking a quick drink of wine.

"What do you mean?" I asked.

"I take what I do very seriously. You realize what we eat has natural chemicals that the human body and brain react to."

"Like celery," I asked.

"Like celery," he answered.

He opened the oven door and rechecked the mounds. "I think they're done."

He took his towel off his shoulder, removed the metal baking tray, and set it on the cutting board. "These look good. Are you ready to try one?"

With a fork in one hand and the knife in the other, he gently slid the knife under the salmon oyster mounds to free them and placed them on the plates.

I wasn't sure how to eat this, waiting for him to begin. Cutting the combination with his fork, he lifted it to his lips, blew on it, and took the first bite.

"Mm, so good. Really good."

I didn't know what to expect. The taste was odd, nothing like I had before. Obviously, Brian knew something I didn't.

Brian watched, "What do you think?"

"Different," I mumbled, "Really different."

"Different, yes different. That's what we were looking for, something different," he proudly exclaimed. "Let's have a toast."

I lifted my glass with Brian and washed down the first bite; in my inebriated state, I wanted to know more.

"Tell me about the secret society, how do I become a player?"

"Janet calls it a game. I call it more than that. I want to know what's happening in the culinary world to be ahead of the game."

He placed the remaining salmon oyster mounds on the empty plates, "Culinary experts have secrets they're not giving up. It's a dog-eat-dog world, no pun intended." Taking another bite and sip, he continued, "Janet and I are well known among these people, and when we travel tasting their work, they become guarded, not letting us in on their secrets."

"I've never heard of such a thing. What part do I play?"

"We need someone unknown that Janet and I can mentor and send out to do clandestine work."

"You mean like a culinary spy?"

"To put it bluntly, yes, like a spy."

"Where does the mentor part come in? Do I go through some kind of training program?"

"Exactly. Janet and I will instruct you, show you the ropes, instruct you how to come up with dynamite recipes that get you into their confidence, then hopefully you can learn their secrets and bring them back here to us."

"Do you have somebody in mind that you want me to go after?"

"We do, and we think you'd be the perfect person to get to her and break her code."

"Her?" I exclaimed. "You mean it's a woman?"

"Her name is Maria. She lives in Chile."

"CHILE!!" I exploded, "What's so special about her?"

"Her father was a German forester hired by the Chilean government to create the timber industry. The government granted him hundreds of acres on the steps of the Andes Mountains, and he gave a portion to Maria where she has a large hacienda and raises llamas."

"She's a German girl?"

"And she's drop dead gorgeous, I don't think getting to know her will be too painful."

"Is she part of this secret culinary society?"

"She is."

"What does she have that you and Janet want?"

"A chili relleno dish nobody has been able to crack. It's an absolute killer and Janet and I want to be the first ones to crack it."

"Do you have any ideas how we're going to be able to do that?"

"I like the way you said 'we're.' Does that mean you're in?"

"I'm in! What's your plan?"

"That we must work on. We better wait for Janet to get back. She's good at producing plans if you know what I mean."

"The devious side of Janet?"

"You know her well."

I wonder how Janet would feel about a younger, gorgeous German girl.

CHAPTER 13

I bolted up from bed with a blaring headache because I drank too much wine. I grasped my head. Still dressed, my mouth felt like a sewer. I tried to figure out what happened last night. I'd gotten flaming drunk over at a gay person's house. I needed a shower, so I turned on the hot water, peeled off my clothes, and nearly scalded myself. I adjusted the water temperature, let it run over my head, and sheet my body while trying to make sense of the last couple of days.

Days ago, I lived with my parents, and now, I have my own place on a houseboat in Sausalito. Mom was right. I was residing amid a bunch of weirdos, lured into a strange relationship with a world-class gay chef and a salacious cougar to become a culinary spy in a secret foodie society. They wanted me to go to Chile to find a recipe for a chili relleno. I didn't even know what a chili relleno was, and in my inebriated state, I'd committed myself to the whole bizarre caper. Had I lost my mind?

After my shower, I thought I'd drive to the stables and saddle up Pickle. I needed something familiar to consider what I was getting myself into.

When I arrived at the stables, James, the caretaker, was cleaning out one of the stalls.

"Morning, James; how are things going?"

"I haven't seen you in a while. Where've you been?"

"I moved into my own place in Sausalito. How's Pickle doing? Thought I'd come on over and take her for a little run."

"She'd love that. She could use the exercise."

I found the saddle and horse blanket where I'd left them in the tack room. Pickle stuck her head out of the upper stall door when she heard me coming and gave a whinny of recognition. I was relieved she hadn't forgotten me.

I set down my load and reached for her to smell me. "Hi, Pickle Girl. You've missed me, haven't you?"

I opened the stall door and reached for the halter on the wall. Placing it over her ears, I led her outside and, with the grooming brush, went to work.

I groomed Pickle to rekindle our relationship before I saddled her up. I rubbed her behind her ears, down her cheeks and throat. She nuzzled my chest as she accepted my affection. I hugged and patted her neck.

"Well, Pickle, I must figure out what I will do with you." I brushed her back and hindquarters. "Mom says I've outgrown you. What do you think, Girl? I think she might be right. We should find someone who loves and cares for you better than me. What do you say we go for a little run, girl? You want to do that?"

Placing the saddle blanket on her back, she knew what was coming and didn't resist. She liked getting out and kicking up her heels. I placed the left stirrup over the horn of the saddle. Pickle turned her head to keep an eye on me. I hoisted the saddle onto her back, adjusted it, and cinched it tight.

I lowered the stirrup off the horn, "You ready to go, girl?"

With the reins in hand, I hoisted myself up into the saddle. When I tugged the reins to the right, she instantly obeyed.

We passed four grazing horses; Pickle and the horses began to speak to each other as if to ask her where she was going. She was excited. Her ears perked up straight forward as she answered the other horses. A little kick on her flanks and she began to canter. Relaxed in the saddle, I let her go to the riverbank.

We slowed to a walk as she went down the steep fifteen-foot bank. I leaned back, my legs stiff in the stirrups.

On the sandy bottom of the dry bed, I gave her another kick, "Let's go, girl," and we went at a full gallop. We maneuvered around bushes and large rocks; I leaned forward as we moved together in harmony. After a good run, we slowed down to a walk.

"Well, girl, I'm not sure why, but I've gotten myself into something, and I'm not sure how it will work out. I won't have time to see you, so I think I better let you go."

We turned back toward the stables, climbed to the harder ground, and took our time getting back. From a small grassy hill with a view of the stables, I viewed the familiar territory I knew as a kid taking riding lessons. Pickle and I had good times, and I loved riding. Now, that has changed. It was time to let Pickle go. A little nudge, and she walked down the hill, back to the trail leading to the stables.

While watching her drink, a lump formed in my throat, and tears welled in my eyes.

After I put her tack away, James came around the corner, "How'd the ride go? You weren't gone long."

"Let me ask you something, James. How much do you think I can get for her?" It wouldn't be fair for me to hang on to her. I'm going in another direction."

"You're not the first person to outgrow his horse. It happens around here. Pickle is a good horse. You could get seven to eight hundred dollars for her. Once word gets out around the stables, she should go fast. I have two girls in mind who would snap her up."

"That'd be great. I'll let my mom know."

"We'll miss you here, but you're doing the right thing."

"Thanks, James, I'll miss everything about this place."

We shook hands and said our goodbyes. I drove off, never to return.

CHAPTER 14

I turned onto Lombard Street and headed up Telegraph Hill, convinced that my decision to part with Pickle was a good one.

I parked in front of my family home and charged through the front door, shouting, "MOM!"

"I'm in the kitchen," she answered.

She was working on a pile of flowers, arranging them in vases to place around the house.

"What brings you here, Sweetie?"

"I went to the stables this morning and rode Pickle."

"How was it?"

I opened the refrigerator door to have a look. "I had a long chat with James and decided to put her up for sale. He thinks finding a good owner for her won't be hard."

"Does he have anybody in mind? There is cake in the cake box."

"He does."

I grabbed a plate, knife, and fork and began working on a chocolate cake, mumbling, "He said there were a couple of young girls who would be perfect for Pickle."

"That sounds like the right decision, Honey."

"The more I think about it, the better I feel."

"I'll tell your father when he gets home. I'm sure he won't object. Oh, I forgot to tell you, you got something in the mail."

"What is it?"

"I'm not sure, something from the government, I think. I'll get it."

I finished my last bite of cake and another gulp of milk as she reentered the kitchen.

"Crazy me, I meant to show it to your father but kept forgetting," she said, laying the brown envelope on the table.

The letter addressed to me had the return address *Selective Service*. Gently fingering the letter, I was afraid to open it.

She arranged her flowers, watching me out of the corner of her eye, "Aren't you going to open it?"

I opened the envelope; I didn't want to read the contents. Painfully, from the top, in full caps, it read:

ORDER TO REPORT FOR ARMED FORCES PHYSICAL EXAMINATION. You must present yourself for the Armed Forces Physical Examination by reporting at the Assembly Room- 17th floor- US Federal Building- East 7th Street- San Francisco CA- On May 18, 1954, at 7 A.M.

I stared at the letter in a semi-catatonic state. I'd known being drafted into the Army was possible, but I had never considered it would happen. Now, in an instant, it was happening. Being a prisoner of the Army was not going to work in my plans of using my allowance to enjoy the pleasures of life. Plus, I just committed to the Secret Culinary Society.

"There must be a way to get out of this?" I mumbled.

"What does it say?"

I couldn't bring myself to tell her. I stood up, took steps toward her, and held out the letter for her to take.

Confused by the official jargon, she looked into my eyes and asked, "What does this mean?"

I came out of shock, "It means," pausing. "I'm likely going to have to go into the Army."

On the way back across the Golden Gate Bridge, my mind kept spinning, and I was unwilling to grasp the reality of what had happened. I kept looking up at the brown envelope tucked in the overhead visor. I needed to talk to Janet. She always had great ideas and could help me put this into perspective.

Parked at the marina, I sat with both fists on the steering wheel. I closed my eyes and pressed my head against my clenched fists. *"Why, why, why?"* kept circulating in my mind.

I looked out to the houseboats serenely moored to the docks, "This place is so cool, and I just got here. Now it's being ripped away from me."

I took hold of the envelope and walked down the gangway where Whiskey was talking to Maud. They both brightened with big smiles.

"Hi, Tony!"

I tried to smile but was unable to. "Hi, Whiskey. Hi, Maud," was the best I could say as I walked past them.

Whiskey squinted, following me down the dock, noticing the brown envelope. He knew what it was. He leaned over to Maud and whispered, "Military draft notice."

"Ooooh," cried Maud, clinching the top of her housecoat, a worried look on her face.

I broke out in a trot, charged over the gangway to the deck, barged in the front door, and set the letter on the bookshelf. I dialed Janet's number. When she picked up the receiver, I blurted out, "JANET!"

"Tony, what's wrong?"

"I received a notice from the draft board to come in for a physical!" I bellowed.

"YOU WHAT?" she screamed. "Oh my God. This is going to fuck up everything!"

"I don't know what to do."

"When do you have to go in?"

"On the eighteenth."

"The eighteenth? That's next week!" she gasped. "Where are you now?"

"I'm at home. Can you come over?"

"Of course. Do you have any food in your house?"

"Shit, I don't know."

"How about wine?"

"Half a bottle."

"I'll get a pizza and wine. It'll take me a bit."

"Thanks. Hurry."

"Try not to worry, Sweetie. I'll get there as soon as I can."

I took the wine out to the deck and poured a hefty glass as the sun set over Marin Headlands. The ducks showed up, quacking for tidbits. I couldn't sit still and walked in circles, in and out of the front door. What was taking Janet so long? Finally, faint footsteps came up the dock, and I ran up the gangway to see Janet.

"Sorry, I'm late. The pizza place was packed."

"I didn't think you'd ever get here. I'm in total agony."

"I know, Sweetie, I'm so sorry."

Janet laid the pizza on the table, opened the wine, and filled two glasses.

"Tell me again, exactly what this letter meant?"

"I'll get it for you, and you can read it yourself."

She studied the letter, reached over, picked up her glass, and took a drink.

"Huh," she said, taking a piece of pizza. "Sweetie, this just says you have to go in for a physical."

"There is nothing wrong with me that I can tell. I think I'm doomed."

"You have flat feet. I heard they don't take guys with flat feet."

"I can't imagine I have anything wrong with my feet."

"Let me ask you this... How do you feel about going into the army?" as she took another bite of her pizza.

After my third piece of pizza, I had a drink and cleared my throat.

"I'm scared." I looked at the ceiling, "I never considered this would happen."

"I think we need to wait and see how things turn out with your physical examination before we take it too seriously."

"I suppose you're right." I leaned back in my chair, watching her finish her pizza.

"You know, Janet, I must tell you something. When I was a kid, my dad took me to the docks right after the war ended. Navy ships came in with crowds of people waiting and bands playing as they tied up the ships."

"I remember those days well," she said.

"I was only ten, standing there holding my dad's hand, and I began to cry as these guys in uniform came down the gangplank."

She saw I was embarrassed, revealing this to her. Tears welled up in her eyes.

"Wives, sweethearts, and families were there, and everybody was crying."

Now, a tear ran down my cheek. It was hard to continue, wiping the tears away, "I've got to tell you, I was so proud that day. I.... I was so proud of those guys."

At a loss for words, Janet continued to look at me, holding her glass on the table.

"One Marine approached me and put his hand out to shake mine. Then he reached into his pocket, pulled out a medal and gave it to me, rubbed my head, and walked off. I watched him until he disappeared into the crowd. You know, I still have that medal."

Now, with tears running down her cheek, "You do? Where is it?"

"It's in my room over at my mom's house. I keep it in a cigar box that my dad gave me so I wouldn't lose it."

"You're saying you'll go in if you pass the physical?"

"I don't have a choice. Do I?"

CHAPTER 15

I took the physical and was rated 1A. Late in the afternoon, I returned to the houseboat with orders for induction into the Army. I had thirty days to sort out my civilian affairs.

I sat on the deckchair, beer in hand, living the dream, but this abrupt change of direction was hard to manage. I heard footsteps on the dock. Whiskey and his dog stood looking at me.

"Permission to come aboard?" Whiskey asked.

I wanted to be alone, but I couldn't refuse. "Sure. Come aboard. Would you like a beer?"

"No, thank you. I quit drinking years ago," Whiskey replied, coming on deck.

"Please sit down." I moved a chair next to mine. "Do you mind if I get another beer?"

"Of course not. I hope I'm not bothering you."

"No bother, give me a second," I lied.

Whiskey's dog sat in his lap, sounding like a cat's purr as Whiskey scratched behind his ear. I took a swig of beer as we silently gazed out over the bay.

Finally, Whiskey spoke, "How'd your physical go?"

Surprised Whisky knew about it, "1A. How did you know?"

"Small place, here. Things get around."

"Of course. Should have known." I said, gently shaking my head.

Breaking the trance of the water, Whiskey continued, "You know I was in the Navy?"

With mild surprise, "No, I didn't."

"Twenty-five years. Traveled the world and got to meet Teddy Roosevelt twice."

Relieved from my own dilemma, I sputtered, "You met Teddy Roosevelt twice? How did that happen?"

"I joined up when I was sixteen. They made me a cook and assigned me to the USS Yucatan."

"What year did they make you a cook?"

"Let's see... That was 1886."

"How old are you, Whiskey?"

"I'm eighty-five this year."

"You're eighty-five?

"Yeah. I was in the Spanish-American War and a lot more than that."

It hadn't occurred to me that anyone from that far back in history could still be alive. I knew the little man was old, but hadn't guessed he was THAT old.

I took a swig of beer, "How did you meet Teddy Roosevelt?"

"Roosevelt was with the Rough Riders, and the Yucatan was part of the convoy that took them to Cuba. He was on our ship. When you work in the galley, you meet everybody."

"I'd never have guessed that in a million years."

"I don't bring it up much. I figured with you going into the Army, I wanted to let you know."

Embarrassed, I took another swig and looked over the water. "You said you met him twice. How did that happen?"

Whiskey pondered briefly, "After the Spanish-American war, Roosevelt became president when President McKinley was assassinated. I made First Class Cook, and the Navy transferred me to the USS Connecticut, part of the Great White Fleet, to enforce Roosevelt's international policy of *Speak softly and carry a big stick*."

"I learned about it in history class. You were a part of that?"

"I was assigned to the Officer's Mess, and before we set sail, Teddy came aboard for dinner to wish us off. I met him there and got to shake his hand. I'll never forget that his favorite foods were pigs in a blanket and fried chicken with white gravy. We made it for him."

I chuckled, "You're kidding,"

"He put seven cubes of sugar in his coffee."

"Seven cubes? Oh my God. How funny." After a pause, "Did you sail with the fleet?"

"I sailed with Commodore Evans, Admiral of the Fleet, worldwide. Quite an experience for a young man. I'm quite proud of it."

Hearing Whiskey's story, I felt small, with nothing to show for myself except climbing to the top of the Golden Gate Bridge and Janet, of course. I had a way to go to match this funny little guy. As Whiskey talked, the fear of entering the Army began draining.

I wanted to hear more from Whiskey, "Were you in World War One?"

"I was. But I didn't do anything. I transferred to the USS Arizona."

I blurted out, "You were on the Arizona!?"

"I was made Chief Petty Officer and put in charge of the Officer's Mess. But we didn't go anywhere. We stayed on the East Coast."

"They kept Arizona on the East Coast? Why was that?"

"From what I understand, they feared the German U-boats and didn't want to lose her. She took me to the Mediterranean after the war on a diplomatic mission. But I never figured out what it was about."

"You went to the Mediterranean?"

"I told you; I got to cover the earth in the Navy. After that trip, I served my twenty-five years and retired. After I got out, the Navy sent her to the Pacific. I was sad I didn't get to go along."

I couldn't help asking the question, "How did you feel when the Japs blew her up at Pearl Harbor?"

Whiskey shook as he raised his voice, "I was madder than hell. I remember everything about that ship. She was beautiful, the pride of the Navy, and the pride of my life. I tried to rejoin and kill every Jap. But they wouldn't take me. I was too old. I cried my eyes out for years after that and still do."

Whiskey placed his hands over his eyes as he tried to hold back the tears.

I felt bad I asked that question and tried to change the subject. "I'm sorry I brought it up, Whiskey. I can't imagine how you feel."

Whiskey gathered his wits, "I get emotional at times. I wanted to see you. Going into the armed forces is a big change in a man's life. I didn't want you to feel alone."

Lost for words, I didn't know what to do or say next.

"I better mosey on. It's time to feed this little dog." Rising from his chair, "We're going to miss you around here even though you weren't here long. We're very proud of you."

Whiskey held out his hand, but I gave him a hug instead, resting my head on his shoulders, "Thanks, Whiskey, I feel better now; I'll never forget it."

The little dog in Whiskey's arms got crushed between us and let out a yip. I released my grip and looked down at the dog, "Sorry, Billy!" I rubbed the dog's head.

"He'll be all right," Whiskey said with a smile. "You'll be around for a while, and Maud wants to give you a going away party. Would you be up for that?"

With my new-found appreciation for the people around me, "That'd be great! I'll ask Janet to help."

"Splendid! Janet knows how to throw a party." Whiskey turned and walked up the gangplank.

.

CHAPTER 16

Everyone was excited about the party. Brian hosted it on his deck, strung with Christmas lights. He made hors d'oeuvres, and Janet brought the alcohol. I arrived late, leaving the others to mingle and chat. Janet, Brian, Whiskey, Harold, and Maud were there.

Whiskey dressed in his usual attire. Maud wore a floor-length silk pink flowered dress, her hair bouffant. Her makeup was orderly and hinted at a time when she was incredibly attractive. It was a shock to see Harold wearing regular trousers without his ass exposed. Whiskey, glass in one hand and leash in the other, sipped an icy glass of orange juice, while everyone else enjoyed alcohol.

When I stepped aboard, Janet brought me a glass of wine, "There you are, Sweetie, the guest of honor."

Maud gave me a big hug and a kiss on the cheek.

Brian took my shoulders, "We're going to miss you, Kid."

Whiskey set down his drink, held out his hand, and said, "Oh hell," and wrapped his free hand around my neck, looking at me, "I'm proud of you, Boy."

Harold stood back, observing.

During the celebration, the conversation turned to Maud. Whiskey addressed the group, "Did you know Maud was a professional dancer?"

We turned to Maud, who looked embarrassed, "Whiskey, you didn't have to bring that up."

"Aw, Maud! I know all your secrets. Why not? It's true."

Then he looked at us and said, "She was one of the original Rockettes when they started in 1925."

"How did that come about?" asked Janet.

"We don't need to go into that," Maud blushed.

"Yes, we do," Brian insisted.

"We want the details. Come on, tell us about it."

Harold stood quietly in the background, smiling.

"If you must know, I was dancing at the Lion's Club in St Louis, a back-alley speakeasy during prohibition."

"How old were you?" I asked, spellbound.

"Seventeen. My mom put me up to it."

"Really?" mused Janet.

Maud finished her third scotch on the rocks, making it easier to share her past.

"Times were hard for most people, especially for women. My mom worked hard during the day and entertained men on the side at night to make ends meet. I hate to bring this up about my poor Mom, but that's how it was."

Mesmerized by Maud's revelation, Brian finished his glass of wine and poured himself another. "This is something we need to know, Maud. Keep going."

"I used to dance around the house to music records my mom had. They were lively tunes. She thought I had talent and asked one of her gentleman friends to get me the job."

Whiskey, who heard it all before, looked content that Maud was the center of attention.

"Mother was a good-looking woman and didn't mess around with riffraff, only high-class gentlemen. They had to have money. Five of the men were mobsters, but they treated her well."

I asked, "What were those speakeasies like?"

She poured herself another scotch, "They were wild places. People dressed up, drank alcohol, and a band played Charleston music. Three other dancers and I danced on stage, wearing almost nothing as the others danced on the dance floor. It was so much fun. None of us girls had a care in the world. I loved it."

I asked, "What about the mob?"

"They controlled everything, but it was no problem for us girls. If you played along, they took care of you."

Janet added, "Of course you had boyfriends."

"Boyfriends! My word, did I have boyfriends? Handsome ones with money. They took me everywhere: to political parties where I met senators and governors and on cruises on luxury yachts. I had the time of my life, never paying for anything."

"Anybody special?" Janet asked.

I thought to myself, *I can't imagine Maud with her smeared lipstick and nightgown being anyone's sex object.*

"Harry Botticelli. He was a member of the mob. I loved him, and he loved me. He is the one that got me on with the Rockettes. He traveled with me wherever the Rockettes went, from the east to the west coast. We traveled together on a tour of Europe. He was a great lover; nobody could match him."

Brian asked, "How did you end up here? I never heard this part of your life."

"A gal's legs won't last forever, and as I got older, my legs began to give out on me. Harry got shot in a run-in with a rival gang and died. I was heartbroken, and I wanted to get away from it. Fortunately, he'd cared for me, and I socked away money. I remembered San Francisco from our travels and came out, found this place, and moved in. So here I am." Maud concluded, finishing her sixth scotch, barely able to stand up.

Whiskey realized Maud had too much to drink and broke into the conversation. "Not to be a party pooper, but it looks like I'd better get Maud home." He took hold of her arm to keep her from falling, his dog pressed to his chest in his other arm.

Saying their goodbyes, Whiskey guided Maud to the gangplank, where she lost her balance and fell back, causing them both to stumble and fall to the deck. Whiskey's dog Billy flew leash and all over the handrail into the bay. Janet, Brian, and I rushed to their aid.

Whiskey shouted, "Billy! Where's Billy?"

I saw the dog struggling in the water, tangled up in the leash. His head disappeared and reappeared at the water's surface. Without thinking, I dove into the bay to save the little guy. None of the others noticed the dog go over the side, and they were shocked by my sudden dive.

Harold sat, his right hand levitating a drink above his elbow, which rested on the railing. His left hand pushed a sandwich into his mouth. He watched the pandemonium in total silence.

Maud mumbled incoherently, rolling on the deck as Janet tried to get her on her feet. Brian pulled Whiskey to his feet. Placing Maud in a chair, Janet turned her head to where I dove in.

"Tony, what in the hell!"

Treading water, I held Billy in the air.

"Oh my God!" cried Whiskey.

Brian rushed to the railing, reached out to take my free hand, and pulled me to the houseboat, taking the dog. He handed Billy to a limping Whiskey. I pulled myself up as Janet rushed into the house to find a towel. She came out as I was dripping on Brian's deck. They speechlessly stared at me except for Maud, who sat in the chair with her chin on her chest and passed out.

Janet wiped me down, "Are you all right, Sweetie? What a brave thing you did."

I began to shiver, "Man, that was cold."

Brian laughed, "Good thing you had that wine in you."

"Oh, shut up, Brian," Janet scolded as she continued to pat me down. Then she lost control and started laughing.

Whiskey wasn't laughing, "Thank you. There is no way I can ever repay you for what you did. I don't know what I'd do without Billy."

I smiled at Whiskey and shivered as Harold walked up the gangplank to head home.

Janet regained her self-control and turned to me, "We'd better get you home in some dry clothes."

"I can manage. You better get Maud into bed," as I glanced at the oblivious Maud, who passed out in the chair.

I shuffled back to my houseboat as the others struggled with Maud. I stripped on the deck and went to the shower, rotating myself in the hot water to melt away the chill. Janet came, lifted off her dress, and squeezed into the tiny shower with me.

"I haven't given you my going away present," and she locked her lips on mine.

CHAPTER 17

I completed eight weeks of boot camp and artillery training at Fort Sill, Oklahoma, before being shipped to Germany. Army life suited me well. I enjoyed the discipline and learning new skills and quickly bonded with my fellow soldiers when we weren't training.

Assigned to H Battery, 105 Howitzers, 5th Field Artillery Unit in Bamberg, Bavaria, I took advantage of the government's all-expense paid trip to Europe.

Letters from Whiskey kept me informed of the latest news at the Marina. During my training, he opened his heart to me in his letters. He'd never married, and his little dog, Billy, was the focus of his heart.

Whiskey wrote that he considered me the closest thing to a son he ever had. His letters had a way of cheering me up during tough situations.

I was truly saddened when he sent me the news that Maud had passed. I thought back to the party going away and hearing about her past life. He wrote that he checked on Maud every morning, and one morning, he found she'd died in her sleep. She had a peaceful look on her face.

He wrote how he took the responsibility of managing her funeral arrangements and had her buried in the Catholic Churchyard of St. Mary, Star of the Sea. Every Sunday, he and Billy walked to the gravesite to visit, but not before buying fresh flowers at Nancy Ann's Flower Market so he could place a fresh bouquet in the urn with the headstone he'd commissioned. He said a prayer for Maud and talked to her as if she could hear and might join in the conversation. He told her everything that was happening at the marina and any changes to the town. He read my letters to her, certain she wanted to know.

He sent me a picture of the granite headstone. I was surprised by the inscription. It said "Maud Weatherby," and below that, "The Dancing Diamond."

I returned to him and asked about the inscription, "The Dancing Diamond?"

"I'll tell you about it later," Whiskey promised.

I was excited when Janet and Brian came to visit. I took time off from my duties and traveled with them, receiving an inside view of the European avant-garde community. She introduced me to people and places hidden from tourists.

Due to the language barrier, I struggled to fit in with the European avant-garde crowd as Janet and Brian wandered among them, talking and laughing with old friends. To cope, I silently followed in their wake, smiling and nodding at appropriate times. These people were so self-absorbed that I didn't have to worry about them asking me a question.

After Brian's culinary gala in Valencia, Spain, I was impressed by how far his influence had traveled from the houseboat in Sausalito.

While in Valencia, Janet and I sat on a bench overlooking the seawall at multimillion-dollar yachts when Janet mentioned, "These are the people we deal with. When you go to Argentina, you'll be around people like this. This is a good introduction for you."

I turned and looked at her and laughed, "Yeah, the people at the Q Club have much catching up to do to match these people."

She looked at me and nodded her head as we laughed together.

"You know Janet, I have a strange feeling about this place. It's like Valencia isn't finished with me yet."

"You never know," she answered. "The world is our playground."

After spending time with Janet and Brian in Europe, I was excited to go to Argentina.

CHAPTER 18

Back on duty with the Army, in the pouring rain, we uncoupled our 105 howitzers from the rear of the deuce and a half truck. The driver's foot slipped from the clutch, causing the truck to lurch forward. None of us were ready for it when the gun trails that stabilize the howitzer during firing fell, crushing my foot.

I fell back in the mud and screamed in agony. The crew instantly lifted the trails to relieve my foot and free me. A cry rang out for the medic. The medic not so tenderly took off my boot as I screamed some more. After he looked at my mangled foot, he shot me in the hip with morphine. The rest was a blur.

I woke up in the army hospital with my foot wrapped up as it hung in a sling, metal pins protruding from the bandage.

Doped up, this seemed like a bad dream as I tried to piece it together. Through blurry eyes, I vaguely remember the doctor standing next to the bed.

"It took three hours to pin and screw your foot back together. It will take time to get right, if ever. I'm recommending you for a medical discharge," he told me.

I was shocked. The news seemed to go over my head until I found myself in the recovery unit at Letterman Army Hospital in San Francisco. After weeks of therapy, I was discharged from the hospital and the Army as well.

CHAPTER 19

I moved in with Janet. We picked up where we left off, hit the clubs, and spent time with Brian. I experienced new dishes and, of course, took time out for lovemaking.

While having wine and cheese, Janet looked over the bay in her condo and revealed her plan.

"My Bohemian friend Dr. Ron Wasson has a doctorate in animal husbandry. He teaches the animal husbandry course at Humboldt State College in Arcata, California. He's interested in South American llamas and has a llama farm near Eureka where he can study them. His main interests are animal diseases and how to find cures."

Then she asked me, "Tony, what would you think about taking a course in animal husbandry at Humboldt State College?"

"Why would I want to do that?" I answered.

"I thought about Ron Wasson, and a light went off in my head. If I brought Dr. Wasson and you together, you could get an understanding of the llamas. It would be a perfect alibi to get you in with Maria at her llama ranch in Chile."

"You think we can make that connection?"

"I do. We can't send you to Chile and have you walk into Maria's ranch and ask for the recipe. She'd never give it to you. If you work with Wasson and learn what you can about llamas, she might greet you with open arms," explained Janet.

"I'm not much of an academic."

"That's not a problem. You only need to learn the right language."

"You're amazing, Janet. Chile in the spring–let's go for it." I answered.

"I'll call Ron and see what we have to do."

We tipped our glasses and polish off the wine. Janet stood, taking my hand. " Are you ready for a nooner?"

She led me into the bedroom, lifted her dress over her head, and tossed it on a chair. "Wasson has been to Chile; I'm sure he knows Maria. I wonder if I can get him on our side. Come on, Sweetie, get your clothes off."

CHAPTER 20

Janet worked it out and got me into the class. She and I drove up to Eureka together to meet Wasson and get acquainted with the area. Wasson was an Army veteran who'd fought in the Korean War, so we hit it off well. He helped me use my GI Bill to pay for the class. I took to llamas readily and enjoyed helping Wasson further his research in the laboratory. He told me about his breakthrough in finding a cure for the hoof and mouth disease FVDV A24. When he asked me to help him take blood and saliva samples from the herd, evaluating the antiviral, I had a legitimate reason and alibi to go to Chile.

When I called Janet, she was ecstatic.

"That's absolutely fantastic!' she yelled. "I knew this plan would work!"

Then she asked me, "How are you coming with Brian's Oyster Salmon Wrap? You need a blowout recipe to impress her."

"I've been working on it. There are plenty of oysters and salmon here on Humboldt Bay. I developed a sauce and invited Wasson over to try the combo. He went apeshit over it."

"That is fantastic, sweetie. This is better than I ever imagined."

Janet came to Eureka, and the three of us went to Waterfront Grill for dinner by the bay. Then, it was time to work out the plan with Ron.

During the pre-dinner drinks, I opened the conversation.

"Ron, what would you think if I went to Chile to study the llama in its natural environment and take blood and saliva samples to see if the antiviral is as effective there as it is here?"

Ron didn't answer right away and looked unsettled as the atmosphere thickened. Janet fiddled with her wine glass.

I took another drink and then continued, "I understand the antiviral is your intellectual property, and I wouldn't go without your authorization and oversight. I'm asking permission; I want to do it after what you taught me."

A little flattery broke the ice. After a pause, he responded, "I see advantages for further research. Can I trust you to fulfill your promise and do the job right?"

Janet joined the conversation. "Tony and I had this conversation a while back." She looked at me and then went back to Wasson.

"Tony appreciates what you've done for him, and it would be fitting for one of your students to follow through and advance this work."

Having planted the seed, we rested it while we enjoyed our meal. The subject changed, and he and Janet chatted about other trivial matters. Wasson asked Janet about her work at the gallery. She filled him in on changes she was making and added that she'd found a couple of new artists and was excited about the possibilities.

The server came and cleared the table, and we ordered after-dinner drinks. Wasson sat back silently in his chair and then raised his eyes.

"I'm warming up to the idea of you going to Chile. I worked with the University of Santiago and know a professor I could put you in contact with. I'd like to go, but the demands of promoting the antiviral stateside would take years before I could venture further. I'll give you the green light. We'll have to sign a contract to keep everything legal."

With a sigh of relief, Janet dug a little deeper, "On your travels to Chile, have you ever met a German girl named Maria Hollman?"

Amused, he looked at Janet and said, "As a matter of fact, I have. How did you know about her?"

"We have mutual friends. I understand she has a llama ranch and hangs out at this fabulous bar on a river."

A sly look on his face, "I can tell you're baiting me, Janet. Why do you want to know?"

"Ron, you know Brian and me; she has a recipe we want."

"Ah, ah, ah," he answered. "There's more to this venture than meets the eye."

"There is." She swished her wine and looked at Wasson.

Wasson bowed his head and laughed, "You are funny, Janet, you and your games. Okay, I'll tell you what I know. I met her and her father at Ricardo's Bar & Hotel on the Cachapoal River. Ricardo's is a well-known establishment that Maria frequents. The Bar hangs over the edge of a cliff overlooking the river with a view of a waterfall on the other side. She always has an entourage, and they party there. There are rooms across the street where I stay during my research. It was a fun getaway."

After the evening with Wasson, Janet and I solidified the plan for me to rent a room from Ricardo and be there when Maria showed up. I had to figure out how to initiate a meeting with her, then wing it to get an invitation to her ranch to crack the code to her chili rellenos.

Chapter 21

The Lockheed Constellation was the most comfortable way to travel from Los Angeles to Chile. Henry, an executive with Pan American Airways, got me on this flight as his guest at no cost.

Before I left, I thought of Whiskey, Billy, and Maud because Whiskey was disappointed. After all, I didn't have a chance to get back to the marina. He wanted to tell me about Maud, so he wrote me a letter. The words jumped off the page as I read it on the flight.

> *Dear Tony,*
>
> *I know Maud seemed a bit eccentric to you, but then, didn't we all? I've told you about her death. She was a friend who grew on me over the years, and Billy and I miss her. Now that she's gone and the fear of revelation has passed, I'd like you to know about her life. She was both simple and complex, but needed to guard her secrets for genuine reasons.*
>
> *She told you something about her lover, Harry Botticelli, but she failed to mention that he was the notorious Harry Botts, a big deal in The Mob. They had a true and loyal love affair, and Harry did everything to keep her happy and safe in a very unsafe world.*
>
> *Back then, everyone knew her by her stage name, 'The Dancing Diamond.' Her mob family called her Diamond, and Harry called her Di.*
>
> *Harry's gang had a piece of the action around St. Louis during the Prohibition. They watched out for rival gangs trying to encroach on their territory. When it happened, the exchanges turned violent. Harry*

raided a rival gang's warehouse, killing two guards and stealing barrels of liquor and a case of cash.

When he discovered this rival gang was associated with the famous Al Capone, he knew his days were numbered. He rushed back to the apartment where he and Di lived and told her to gather her things. Her life was in danger, not only from Capone but also from the police, paid by Capone. She was associated with Harry and knew all his secrets.

They raced to the train station, and he bought her a ticket to San Francisco, where his sister lived. He told her he'd have his sister pick her up and find her a place to stay until the situation settled, and they would meet again. At the station, Harry gave her the case full of money he had stolen from Capone to keep until they got back together.

When she arrived, Harry's sister met her, took her to the Marina, and put her in the houseboat. Within hours, she got news that Harry was shot and killed by Al Capone's henchmen. She was devastated, but hard and brilliant as a diamond.

She'd gone by Diamond for so long that nobody knew her real name. So, she became Maud again, hiding in plain sight under her real name. She stayed put, found a guy to set her up with investments, and, with the cash, lived a quiet life until her death.

After she died, I was in her house to sort things out and found the case that Harry had given her, still half full of cash. There was also a scrapbook with old photos and newspaper clippings. She was a real stunner. With the money I found, I paid for the burial arrangements and gave the rest to charity.

I did the best I knew how. I don't know what became of Harry's sister. I'm guessing she and Maud didn't have a relationship. The less known, the safer, removed from danger, I think. Anyway, those gangsters are long gone, but after so many years of hiding, it became a habit, fearing that someone might be out there looking for her. So, now you know.

Enjoy your trip and Good Luck! Yours, Jack (Whiskey)

The old stories of gangsters and prohibition were like a movie. I thought of the first time I saw Maud walking down the dock to meet me in her night clothes and smeared lipstick. Who would have known she was a dancer and love of a mob boss?

While on the houseboat, I appreciated Maud as a real person. It was amusing to rub elbows with such a colorful character, and I would miss her.

Chapter 22

The ground crew at Santiago Airport rolled the stairway up to Flight 37 from Los Angeles, opening the Constellation's door for the passengers to exit after the extended flight.

It was a warm, sunny day in Santiago as I stepped onto the tarmac and followed the rest of the passengers into the terminal. Over the door read Aduana/Control de Pasaportes. My passport and entry visa were in the upper right-hand pocket of my shirt. In my left pocket, I had a map folded up with directions to Ricardo's Bar and Hotel on the Cachapoal River.

In the Army, I learned to travel light, so the only luggage I needed was a small knapsack with the essentials for an extended stay.

After clearing customs, I went to the currency exchange desk to exchange $50.00 for 33,800 Chilean pesos and then went outside to find a taxi.

A crowd outside waited to meet the incoming passengers from Flight 37. I worked through the crowd to a row of taxis; a young boy ran up, "Taxi, Senor?"

"Si," I responded.

The boy took me to a red four-door 1953 Chevrolet taxi and opened the back door. I acknowledged the driver and tossed my pack in the back. I took a coin out of my pocket, not knowing the denomination, and handed it to the boy. He didn't look at it when he put it in his pocket and ran back to grab another customer.

The driver asked in Spanish where I was going.

"San Borja Bus Station," I replied.

The two-lane road from the airport to the bus station was newly paved. The driver turned right and went half a block with the main train station on the left and the San Borja bus terminal on the right.

Traffic was congested. The driver double-parked in front of the terminal. He looked back at me and said, "Dos mil quinientos."

"Twenty-five hundred pesos," I repeated in English, handing three thousand pesos to the driver. Keep the change."

I struggled through the crowd to enter the terminal, which was as crowded inside as outside. The ticket windows on the back wall had no defined lines to get to them. People pushed their way forward until they made it to the ticket window. Entering the fray and taking small steps, I began to move forward. After twenty minutes, within a short distance of one of the windows, people kept trying to crowd in front of me. I moved my weight around to fend them off and maintain my position in front of the window.

In my ruptured Spanish, "Una boleta para-Coya."

The balding, round-faced teller, who had glasses at the end of his nose, looked over his glasses and said, " Dos mil quinientos."

I received a ticket to Coya on bus number 17, departing at 1300. I checked my watch; it was a quarter to twelve.

The staging area was surrounded by a white ten-foot-high block wall with numbered parking spaces for forty buses—even numbers on the one side of the terminal and odd numbers on the other side.

Buses, school buses, and modern coaches were parked in their spaces. Around the buses, there was a flourish of activity as drivers and their assistants loaded large bags and boxes on top of the bus in metal luggage racks. The assistants guided the buses back out.

Bus Seventeen, an odd number, would be on the far side. I walked along the block wall lined with benches. Space #17 was empty; there was no bus. People waited. Older ladies, three nuns, and children sat on the benches.

I turned to an older man and showed him my ticket, "Este bus para-Coya?"

The man looked up, "Si. Este es el bus para-Coya."

A small girl wearing a colorful apron approached with a bag of oranges. I hadn't eaten since I got off the plane and bought three oranges to have later.

A silver coach arrived, passed the #17 parking space, and stopped. The assistant came out, walked to the rear, and directed the coach to our slip.

The newly arrived passengers got off the bus and milled around while the assistant opened the baggage hatches and found their luggage. The driver got out and went into the terminal. I was first in line to get on the bus, but stopped by the assistant, who boarded the bus to clean up the trash left behind. I realized it might take a while before they let us on, so I reached into my pack and pulled out an orange.

Minutes later, the assistant reemerged with a basket full of trash. He closed the door and disappeared into the terminal.

After I ate my third orange, the man reappeared with a trolley of packages and loaded them into the cargo hold. When he was finished, he gestured for people to bring their luggage and looked at their tickets before he loaded their goods into the hold. I kept my knapsack.

The assistant closed the cargo hatches and waved to the nuns at the entry door to come to the front of the group. I felt embarrassed as I pushed back against the crowd to make room for them. He let them on board without checking their tickets, allowing passengers to force their way in front of me.

I realized I'd have to be aggressive to regain a place in line and pressed forward as others pushed to get on the bus. After eight passengers squeezed in front of me, the assistant reached for my ticket and let me board. The three nuns sat in the front row; I moved down the aisle, found two empty seats, and slid into the window seat.

A mother with two children sat in the seats across the aisle, and a young boy took the seat next to me. The children were well-mannered and sat quietly. I looked down at the boy, and he smiled and looked over at his mother, who looked at me and smiled. I smiled back.

The driver got on board, took the last few gulps from a can of beer, and then placed a fresh can in a cup holder on the dashboard. He started the engine and let it idle as he opened the other can of beer and took a swallow.

CHAPTER 23

I couldn't take my eyes off the towering white mountains during the hour-and-a-half-hour ride from Santiago to Coya. It was five-thirty in the afternoon when I stepped from the bus and moved out of the way to get my bearings. The town center had old colonial buildings lining each side of the main street. A white cathedral flanked by twin bell towers stood at the center. The town itself was nestled in a green forested valley surrounded by towering snow-topped mountains. The landscape was rugged, broken up by steep ravines. A rushing river flowed to the right. I was in the right place.

As the sun set, the air became slightly chillier. Ricardo's Place wasn't far out of town, and I hoped to get there before dark. Taxis parked on the main road, and the drivers leaned on the fenders. With my pack over my shoulder, I headed toward them.

One of the drivers stood up, "Taxi, Señor?"

"Yes, please." Then I remembered my Spanish, "Si, Señor."

The driver opened the back door, "Donde vas?"

"Ricardo's Bar."

The driver thought momentarily, "Ricardo's, al otro lado de la cascade?"

I pulled out the map with markings to Ricardo's and wrote Highway 265 East on it. The driver headed east through town. When we got to the cathedral, he turned right. A road sign read H265, so I was confident we were headed in the right direction.

A wooden bridge crossed over a stream that flowed into the Cachapoal River. Ahead were lights. The driver slowed down and stopped in front of a building on the right with a sign over the door 'Ricardo's Bar.' The front of the bar had a covered porch lined with colorful Christmas lights, chairs spaced along it, and a large wooden double door lit up with a white light overhead. Across the road were eight matching bungalows in a row. Light shone through the curtains.

The driver came around and opened the door, "Ricardo's Bar, Señor."

I paid the driver along with a tip.

I entered the double doors into a ten-foot by ten-foot foyer. Family photos hung from the walls. The dimly lit seating area, with the bar on the left, had tables scattered around a wooden floor. The back walls had windows that looked across the river to a waterfall cascading on the other side.

Two couples were having drinks near the window, enjoying the view. The building extended over a cliff, with the river below. I looked for the bartender and took a seat at the empty bar.

Behind the bar was a counter with a porcelain sink in the middle. The passageway to the dining area was on the far side.

A mirror hung on the wall behind the bar. On either side were shelves filled with beer and wine glasses. Above the mirror were types of bottled beer, most of which I didn't recognize. Half doors swung into the kitchen. The whole establishment looked tidy and clean. I was glad to be there.

I was looking out the windows at the falls when the kitchen door squeaked open. A man in his mid-thirties approached me and placed his hand on the bar. His black hair was slicked back, and he was clean-shaven with dark eyes and thick eyebrows. Black trousers and a black long-sleeved shirt buttoned at the collar were tucked in his belt, and a towel hung down to mid-thigh.

"Buenas Noches, Señor. ¿Cómo puedo conseguir que ayudará?"

The first words out of my mouth were, "Do you speak English?"

He stood up straight and wiped his hands, "You're an American I assume?"

I nodded, "I am."

"Welcome to Chile and Ricardo's Bar. What can I get you?"

"What beer do you suggest?"

"Escudo is the Chilean beer. Would you like to try it?"

"That would be great, thank you."

He poured the beer into the glass and asked, "Where are you from in the States?"

"California."

"California. My name is Alec. What's yours?"

"Tony. Nice to meet you," shaking Alec's hand.

"Nice to meet you, too, Tony. Try the beer and tell me what you think."

Leaving a little froth on my upper lip, I wiped my mouth, "Very good! Just what I needed. I came in from Santiago today."

From under the bar, he placed a napkin and a bowl of nuts in front of me. I reached for the nuts.

"Is there anything else I can get you?" he asked.

"I'll take another beer. Do you serve food here?"

"Would you like to see a menu?"

"Thanks, I would," and reached for more nuts.

On the menu was a list of empanadas.

"What are these empanadas?"

"Empanadas are different seasoned meats wrapped in a roll, covered with our home-made gravy."

"What kind of meat?"

"We have beef, of course, lamb, llama, and chicken."

"Does anything come with them?"

"Black bean soup."

"I'll try the beef with the soup."

Alec placed another glass of beer on the bar and turned to the kitchen before I stopped him. "The rooms across the street—do you have one available for a couple of days?"

"I have three available."

"I'll take one. Do you take U.S. dollars?"

"We do; I'll be right back with your soup."

I started my second beer and thought about what an aesthetic and unique place it was. I wondered who Alec was, where Ricardo might be, and how Alec could speak such good English.

Alec returned with a bowl of black bean soup and placed it before me with silverware on a fresh napkin.

"How are you set for beer?"

"Good for now."

Alec gave a thumbs-up and went to check on his other guests.

A whiff of steam came off the soup. I lifted the hot soup to my lips. The soup was thick and savory and being famished made it all the better.

Alec returned to the bar, opened a bottle of red wine, poured two glasses, and served them to two other guests. When he returned, I finished the soup and washed it down with beer.

Alec soon came out from the kitchen with the empanadas. The gravy steamed with an enticing aroma.

He placed the plate in front of me, "Another beer?"

"Please. They sure smell good."

Alec smiled, "I think you'll enjoy it." He poured another beer and returned to the kitchen.

The empanadas were filled with shredded beef. Hungry as I was, it didn't take long for me to finish the whole plate and half of the beer.

My hunger was satisfied, and my thoughts turned to the mission at hand: how to meet Maria. The door to Maria could be through Alec, but I'd have to cultivate a conversation to pull off this ruse. Based on our conversation, it wouldn't be hard to do.

"How was it?" asked Alec as he retrieved the plate and silverware.

"Filled the spot, thanks. I was wondering," I asked, "Where is Ricardo?"

"Ricardo! Ricardo passed away four years ago. He built this place and the rooms across the street from the ground up."

Stunned by the news, "I'm sorry, I didn't know. Who owns this place now?"

"His daughter, Manuela, took it over."

"She does an excellent job keeping it up. Where is she now?"

Alec laughed, "She's in Spain."

"Spain! What does she do there?"

"She has family there and goes once a year for a few months."

"Do you work here full time?"

"For right now; she's my cousin."

"That's convenient, keep it in the family."

Alec smirked and shook his head yes.

"I have one more question."

"What's that?" Alec returned.

"How did you learn such good English?"

Alec laughed again, "My parents live in Chicago. I lived there and went to Northwestern University."

"Your family gets around."

"We do," Alec laughed again.

"What was your major at Northwestern?"

"You said one more question."

"I know, but I'm curious."

"I have to check in with my other customers, I'll get back to you in a moment."

It was clear how to pull the trigger on this caper: I would keep the conversation with Alec long enough for him to ask me a question. Beer in hand, I turned the bar stool to watch Alec place a bill on the table of the couple who had finished a bottle of wine. He returned around the bar and put the bill in the trash bin under it.

He came over to me, "Where were we?"

"I asked you what you majored at Northwestern?"

"I completed a BA in business."

"You didn't plan to use your BA in the States?"

"I did, but Manuela called me and asked if I'd come down here and help her with this place."

"You must like it down here?"

"I do, plus the family has other interests that I help with. So, running this place along with the others keeps me busy."

"I guess so. I find this intriguing."

"You think so? Chile is a beautiful place, and the people here are hardworking family-oriented friendly types. The only problem is one must face an earthquake now and again."

We laughed; Alec excused himself to collect the bill from the two getting up to leave.

I watched the couple and Alec chat through the mirror behind the bar. Something he said made them laugh. The man patted Alec on the back and the girl hugged him and kissed on the cheek. They left the table, and Alec wiped and rearranged it, picked up the two empty wine glasses, and returned to the bar, placing them in the sink. He washed and dried them before putting them in the glass rack.

Alec looked at my beer bottle and noticed it was half full, "Now it's my turn. What brings you down here to Chile and Ricardo's Bar?"

Bingo! Now was my chance.

"I'm here on a grant from Humboldt State College, working alongside Santiago University doing research."

"Research? What kind of research? For some kind of degree?"

Alec was hooked, so I had to reel him in with, "No degree; I'm an assistant for Dr. Ron Wasson in the Animal Husbandry Department."

"Animal Husbandry; what kind of animals are you doing research on?"

"Cattle and llamas."

Back at the bar, he leaned forward. "So, what are you doing?"

"I'm taking saliva and blood samples."

With keen interest, he asked, "Do you mind if I ask you what these samples are for?"

Now that I had him, I thought I'd better be a bit elusive and not seem anxious. I needed to let Alec draw me out.

"It's complicated, if I got too much into it, I'd bore you to death."

There was a pause. Alec took another beer from the fridge, opened it, and placed it before me. "This one is on the house. I'd like to know what your research is looking for."

With the four beers going to my head, I'd have to pace myself with the fifth.

"Why are you so interested?" trying to be as polite and nonchalant as the beers would allow.

"You are in the heart of llama and cattle country. My family has a small herd of cattle, plus Manuela has a dear friend that comes here who has a large ranchero up the road raising varied species of llamas and we're struggling with hoof and mouth disease." He paused, "Would your research be in hoof and mouth disease?"

"FMDV A24, to be exact."

"FMDV A24, I'm assuming A24 is the strain of the virus?"

"That's correct."

Alec had more going for him than tending bar at Ricardo's. I tried to change the subject to slow things down.

"This is such a cool place. I'm amazed there aren't more people here."

Alec stood up straight and ran his fingers through his hair.

"Don't worry, Latins never eat early. By nine-thirty this place is full. I can tell you're not too familiar with Latin culture."

"I thought I was. We have Mexicans in California, although I never spent time with them."

"We take a siesta between two and four, get up, do a little more work, and then the families go for a stroll as the sun goes down. Dinner comes late. After that, they hit the drinking establishments until 2 a.m. and sometimes later."

"When do you close?"

"Close…we never close."

"You never close? When do you sleep?"

"I head across the street when things slow down, but we have somebody here all the time."

"You do this all the time?"

"Only when Manuela is in Europe. When she gets back, she takes over. We have an extended family. Everybody pitches in."

"You have a strong family bond."

"That's part of the Latin culture."

"That's impressive."

I finished my beer, "Do you mind showing me my room? I'd like to settle in."

"I'll get your key and take you over there."

Alec rushed into the kitchen and returned with a key tied to a small block of wood with the number 6 on it.

He came from behind the bar, "Follow me."

I picked up my knapsack and went to the front door, where Alec held it open.

We stepped down the lighted porch to the street. I looked up at the cloudless sky and marveled at the stars.

"The stars sure are bright down here."

"They are. Look back over there, you can see the Southern Cross."

I got my first glimpse of the Southern Cross from the middle of the street.

Alec continued, "You don't see that up in your area, but for centuries sailors have navigated by it. It's almost due south as the North Star is due North. Besides that, it gives comfort to those in the area."

"How's that?"

"Because it comes up every night and stays right there. If it hasn't moved, we know everything is safe."

"I guess so," I laughed.

CHAPTER 24

Across the street, Alec put the key into the lock. I admired the door's craftsmanship. The dark wood was hand-carved, and the decorative black hinges extended fully across the door.

"Nice door, where did you find these?" I asked.

"One of Ricardo's talents."

"Too bad I'll never get a chance to meet him."

"He was incredibly talented and the family patriarch. He's well missed by those who knew him, especially the family."

Inside the room, he turned on a light below a ceiling fan.

My attention focused on a llama-skin rug on the terracotta floor. The off-white room had local paintings on the walls and a four-poster double bed. A colorful local Indian-design bedspread, with two fluffy pillows up against the wooden headboard, carved with the same design as the front door, complemented the room.

"I take it Ricardo made the beds also?" I asked.

"Exactly."

He handed me the key and hesitated, "May I ask what your schedule is?"

"My schedule... I'm under the gun really, they've got my time tight. Why do you ask?"

"It would be great if you met my cousin's friend Maria. I know she could use your input."

I paused to manage my response. "I came out to visit Ricardo's place hearing about the waterfall. I wasn't planning an extended stay."

"I can only imagine how pressured you are. You'd not only be helping her, but many more in the region."

"I don't know what to say. It would be a pleasure to meet her, but I'd have to rearrange my schedule and I'm not sure how to go about meeting her."

"That you leave to me. She comes here often. I'll see if she can come tomorrow. Once I tell her of the work you do, I think she'd be more than willing. Give me a couple of moments to work things out and I'll be over."

Alec closed the door. I sat on the edge of the bed, thinking this was too easy. With my hands behind my head, I lay back to ponder as the ceiling fan turned, wafting cool air on my face.

Alec went to the phone and dialed Maria's number. It took a while before Henny, Maria's assistant, answered, "Hello?"

"Henny, this is Alec."

"Hi Alec. How are you?"

"I'm doing well, thank you. Is Maria around?"

"She is. I'll get her for you?"

"Thank you. Tell her it's important."

Alec waited patiently as the minutes ticked by before Maria answered the phone.

"Hi, Alec, what's so important?" Maria asked.

"There's an American guy here who is from Humboldt College doing a study on FMDV. It looks like he might have a cure."

"That sounds interesting. How do I meet this guy?"

"That's why I'm calling. He's here for the night; I'm trying to convince him to stay until tomorrow. I told him he needs to meet you."

"I want to meet this guy, Alec. When do we find out if he is available?"

"I hope he is coming over to use the phone here to talk to his people."

"I can come tomorrow. Let me know if it works for him and get back to me."

"I'll get back to you tonight, but it might be late."

"Don't worry about that. You know how things go around here. I'll wait for your call."

"Talk to you soon, Maria."

CHAPTER 25

After a shower, I felt better and put on fresh clothes. Cars were parked on either side as I crossed to the restaurant. The bar stools had people in lively conversation and laughter. The tables had separate groups for drinking and eating. An attractive young girl waited on the tables. Alec was nowhere in sight.

I took the stool on the far end of the bar. Alec came out of the kitchen and passed me, carrying plates of food. He didn't acknowledge my presence as he served a table of four. He lingered with the foursome and made conversation. When he returned, he noticed me.

"Tony, hang on."

He went to a tub filled with ice and beer, took a beer, opened it, and placed it in front of me. "I was wondering what happened to you," he said.

"I took a shower."

"Figured that. See what I mean? This place fills up around ten."

"I see that."

"Give me a second. I have something to tell you."

He checked on people at the bar, refreshed wine glasses, opened beers, and placed them on the bar. Before he came back, he fixed a couple of mixed drinks.

"I got hold of Maria. She'd love to get together tomorrow if you're going to be around. She can come tomorrow afternoon."

I drank while Alec returned to the kitchen. He came back with a plate of small tortillas and what looked like a mound of feta cheese. He held a small bowl of green enchilada sauce in his other hand. He placed the plates in front of me.

"Try these and see what you think," and handed me a spoon to spread the cheese.

I spread a helping of cheese on the tortillas, dipped the spoon in the sauce, and dribbled it on the cheese. I rolled up the tortilla and took a bite. I couldn't recognize the flavor and looked at Alec.

"Don't tell me, this is llama cheese?"

"Good guess, you like it?"

"Very tasty, thanks," I took another bite. "What do you call these?"

"Quesadilla."

"Quesadilla. I'm going to have to remember that one."

"Are you going to be around tomorrow?"

"I thought about it, and I can work it out. Do you know what time?"

"She shows up around four o'clock and will have people with her. They'll have a party. It's a fun group and I think you will enjoy it."

"I'm sure I will. When I get up in the morning, I'd like to go hiking to check out the surroundings. Do you know a good hiking trail?"

"Follow the road to the right. In a quarter of a mile, you'll find a trail that goes up the mountain. It's well defined and used, there is a small parking area. You won't miss it. It gets steep at times, but when you get to the top, you'll have a magnificent view of the area."

"Sounds perfect. I'm going back to my room and going to bed. Thanks for your help."

"Don't blame you. We're open for breakfast if you want a bite to eat before you head out. And make sure you take water with you on your hike."

"I would, but I didn't bring a canteen."

"I won't be here in the morning, but I'll leave a leather flask for you with water when you come to breakfast. How does that sound?"

"You couldn't be more kind."

We shook hands, and then I turned to leave. "Take the rest of these quesadillas with you in case you get hungry at night. On your hike, when you get higher, look across to the waterfall. You might find something that will surprise you."

"Any hints?"

"I'll let you figure it out."

I thought about the day and how it came down. I was proud of myself but anxious about what would come. This was a game; I would feel stupid if I was found out. I had to play this ruse out, whatever might come. Maria and Alec were part of the game, and if caught, I figured they would take it in stride. This thought eased my mind as I undressed, pulled back the covers, and crawled under the sheets.

CHAPTER 26

I woke up at 7:30 and slept so well that I had to figure out where I was. It came back to me: I was going on a hike, and later, I had a date with Maria. I dressed for the day and looked forward to this hike to check out the countryside. But first, I needed breakfast.

An older lady came to the bar, who I later learned was Alec's aunt. After I gave her my order of Huevos Rancheros, I could see the waterfall in full daylight. This is an incredible place, I thought. Ricardo's imagination to build an edifice hanging over a cliff with such a view should be one of the wonders of the world.

Alec's aunt brought me breakfast, and I poured a good helping of hot sauce over the top and washed my first bite with coffee.

These were such nice people, and the dishonesty of the mission weighed on me. But now I had no choice but to go through with it.

The lady brought a round leather canteen filled with water, which Alec had promised.

"The water. Gracias, how much do I owe you?"

"Nothing, a gift from Alec." she said in English.

She handed me the canteen, and I thanked her again with a tinge of guilt.

The day was bright and sunny, but cool. I stopped by my room to get a sweater and hat, where I noticed the quesadilla on the bedside table. I brought it along in case I got hungry later.

I crossed the road and viewed the falls. I also got a better look at the restaurant's foundation that hung over the cliff. I wondered how he held that restaurant to the cliff.

I looked down at the river to a series of rapids. At the base of the falls was a pool, and I wondered if there might be fish in the river.

I found the trail going up the mountain with switchbacks for a couple of hundred feet and then angled up to the right until it went out of sight.

"This is going to be a challenge," I thought.

The start of the trail had concrete steps. Looking up at the first switchback, I hoped my wounded foot would survive going up this trail. The path went to the right for a hundred feet before turning left. It was well maintained. Was this another brainchild of Ricardo's? Climbing the steps, I wouldn't need my sweater for long. I started sweating like a pig.

The angles of the switchbacks weren't steep and easy to climb. After the last switchback, the trail meandered along the side of the hill for a reasonable distance. I stopped to get my bearings and took a drink from the canteen. There was a better view of the gorge and waterfall. The stream on the other side of the gorge that fed the waterfall flows straight down a gently sloped plateau. Although it was misty, I saw the town of Coya down the valley.

The higher I went, the broader the view below. Gazing down, there was something strange about the stream that fed the falls. It wasn't a meandering stream like most, but a straight ditch. I wondered how this stream could be so straight.

With snow capped peaks of the Andes Mountain range to the east, I imagined the view at the top and quickened my pace.

Finally, I was shocked at the summit, not at the view of the Andes or the valley below, but that someone had brought up two concrete tables with molded benches. How could someone manage these heavy items to the summit? Staring at them, I shook my head.

Between the tables sat a concrete barbeque and a place to set up tents if one wanted to camp out. What foresight. Was this Ricardo's doing? Is this what Alec was talking about, or something else?

I sat on one of the tables and laid back to catch my breath, turning my head toward the high Andes. They swallowed me alive. The towering, majestic mass of bright white peaks and shadowed valleys demanded respect. I'd been to the Rockies, but these were different, a different feel, a different spirit.

I sat up and looked down on Ricardo's, the gorge, and the waterfall. I could make them out clearly. Studying the creek that fed the falls as far as it went, it came out of the same river it flowed into. Someone had built a diversion dam and dug a ditch that allowed the water to flow up the river to the falls. That's why the creek was so straight. This whole scene is manufactured!

Suddenly, I knew what Alec was talking about. This must have been Ricardo's dream: the Restaurant bar hanging over a cliff, the rooms across the street with the hand-carved doors and woodwork. The waterfall across the gorge looked natural from the bar window. The trail and campground at the top of the mountain was Ricardo's. I couldn't imagine the work done to accomplish this personal vision. It was hard, back-breaking work with picks and shovels, concrete, and steel. Taking in the panoramic view of this quality, it fit in like it was supposed to be there. I understood why Alec liked it here and why he came down from Chicago to help. I appreciated the family's commitment to keep this place alive. Ricardo's vision was worth the extraordinary effort shared by the family well after his death. This was a destination worthy of the avant-garde posh trying to steal each other's recipes, a part of the game.

I finished off the last of the quesadilla and took a drink from the canteen. Before starting the descent, I took one last panoramic look, "Such a beautiful place!" Checking my watch, it was a quarter to one. In three hours and fifteen minutes, I'd meet Maria.

It took an hour to get back to my room. Exhausted from the hike, I took a shower. I had everything I needed, and my backstory was so sound that I could impact this country's llama and cattle industry. If all else failed, the trip would be worth it. I lay on the bed and drifted off to sleep.

Chapter 27

Maria and her entourage were in high spirits, with shouts and laughter entering Ricardo's main door. The party started when Henny, Maria's diminutive Chinese assistant, went to the stereo and placed a record on the turntable. Hot Latin music brought the room to life. Two French guys headed for the far side of the bar, checking out the wine. Quickly, they selected a couple of bottles, opened them, and raised them in the air as they danced around the bar. They passed out glasses to the young women who were dancing seductively.

Squeals of laughter mixed with the music. Maria was in the middle of it, but out of the corner of her eye, she was searching, wondering if the man she had come to meet was in the room.

Maria approached the bar while Alec served other customers, "Where is this man I'm supposed to meet?"

A concerned look on his face, "I'm not sure. He told me last night he was going for a hike. I wonder if he's gotten back yet. I hope he is all right."

With twisted lips, she held out her glass for Alec to add more wine, "I hope so, too."

I looked out the window at the parked Land Rovers. The party was underway. I put on a fresh pair of Levi jeans and a long-sleeved khaki shirt, rolling up the sleeves to my elbows, and slipped into clean socks and desert boots. Taking stock of myself in the bathroom mirror, "Okay, let's make this fun." On the way out, I slung a sweater over my shoulders, tying the arms in the front.

Stirred by the music, I crossed the street. I controlled myself to be casual when entering the bar. From the foyer, I saw Maria's group dancing and making noise. I slipped into the first stool open and sat down facing the bar.

Calmly, I sat with my hands folded. I watched Alec work his way down. Through the mirror, I picked out Maria, who was drinking with her group and looking at the waterfall. When Alec spotted me from the corner of his eye, he rushed over.

"I was worried about you. How was the hike?"

"Unbelievable! I saw what you were talking about. My first question, did Ricardo do all of it?"

"He did. Amazing, eh?"

"More than amazing."

"What can I get you to drink?"

"Do you have bourbon?"

"I do"

"I'll have a bourbon seven on ice."

"Coming up."

I spun around and glanced at Maria. Everything they said about her was true.

I was careful not to stare. She wore a black flat-brimmed stovepipe hat seductively tilted forward, partially covering straight, long brownish hair. The poncho of Indian design, striped with black, blue, red, and white, formed a V in the front. Her pants were tight denim tucked into black, silver studded cowboy boots. She had a commanding and confident appearance and a beautiful face. Her body was not delicate, but sound and shapely. She held a glass of wine with both hands in front of her, patiently listening to those around her.

I turned back; I stealthily watched her in the mirror behind the bar.

Alec brought me my drink. "Have you picked out Maria?" he asked.

"The black hat?"

"She's looking forward to meeting you. Have your drink and I'll get her."

I followed Alec in the mirror as he rounded the bar and approached Maria's group. He hesitated a moment for them to finish their conversation. Then, he leaned forward to her ear, and she instantly scanned the bar and focused on me. The other girls looked in my direction as I sipped my drink.

Alec led her toward me, her entourage looking on in interest.

I stood up with a drink in my hand, and our eyes met. Magic struck. Something happened, something I'd never felt before.

Before Alec introduced us, she took charge: "Tony, it's so nice to meet you. I'm Maria. Alec told me about you. Welcome to Chile."

"Thank you, I heard about Ricardo's place and had to come see it."

"You went to the top of the mountain today. You must have gotten the total view."

"I was amazed, but the hike wore me out."

"It does that. How long are you here for?"

"That depends. I'm working on a project with Santiago University, and they've got my schedule tight."

"Alec said you were taking blood and saliva samples for hoof and mouth disease."

"That's right."

"Do you mind if we sit down at a table? I'd like to talk to you."

"Not at all. You lead the way."

Alec raised his hand, "Tony, you want another drink?"

I turned and nodded, holding my drink above my head.

She picked a table by the window. We drew out our chairs. Maria's perfume emitted a delightful scent, and I couldn't resist mentioning it.

"What's that perfume you're wearing?"

She didn't respond immediately, removing her hat and placing it on the table. She looked up and ran her fingers through her hair.

"Thank you. It's something my father bought me years ago."

"Your father, does he live here also?"

"He died six years ago."

"I'm sorry to hear that."

"Thank you. I was close to him."

I played the part and asked, "What did he do?"

"He had a contract with the Chilean Government to establish their forestry program."

"That's a big job. I'm sure he was successful."

"Yes, he was. That's why I'm here. He brought me here as a child and I grew up here. This is my home."

"I understand you own a ranch and raise llamas."

"I suppose Alec has filled you in," Maria said.

"A little bit. He seems very fond of you."

"We're good friends. We grew up with the whole family, his cousin Manuela and me. Did he tell you about Manuela?"

"He gave me a little run down on Ricardo's history. She is in Spain now?" I asked.

"She goes there every year. She is what I consider my best friend."

I could not take my eyes off her face. For a woman who ran a llama ranch, her complexion was flawless. If she had any makeup on, it was hard to tell. Her features had a simple beauty, a girlish, angelic look, and nothing was added or taken away to enhance her beauty. She was gorgeous.

Alec brought fresh drinks in one hand and a bottle of wine in the other. He set them down on the table with a napkin and topped off Maria's glass. I looked up at him and realized I had to get something in my stomach, or the alcohol would dull my senses.

I prodded Alec, "Sorry to bother you, but I need something to eat."

Before Alec could respond, Maria broke in, "Don't worry about that. We have two large paellas coming. You're welcome to join us."

"They should be ready in fifteen minutes," answered Alec.

"Thank you, I'm not sure what a paella is, but thank you."

Alec returned to the bar while Maria explained, "It's a typical Spanish mixture of rice and seafood. I'm sure you will love it."

"Sounds great."

"Now it's my turn," she began. "I'm really interested in what you're doing. How is it you came here?"

"After a stint in the Army, I took an animal husbandry course at Humboldt State College under Professor Ron Wasson."

"You were in the Army?"

"I was, but received a medical discharge after injuring my foot."

"What was your interest in llamas?"

"Ron Wasson."

"That's interesting. I've met Ron, in fact it was here where I met him."

"How long ago was that?"

"It must have been over six years ago, I was still in school, and I was having dinner with my father... but go on."

"I helped Ron at his llama ranch. I got more involved with his research, and he taught me how to take blood and saliva samples and preserve them. When he found a cure with FMDV A24, he wanted to know if the same antiviral would be suitable in South America, so here I am."

"Alec is bringing out the paella. We'd better get you something to eat."

Alec placed the two platters on a table in the center of the room. The group quickly dug into the mixture, with the two French guys being the first to do so.

I helped myself to the paella and considered what I had told Maria, wondering if the alibi had any holes. Was she taking the bait? Another frightening thought lurked: had I fallen in love at first sight?

Maria introduced me to others in her entourage; there was no way I would remember their names. It seemed they knew why I was there. The English lady, Clare, was most inquisitive and bombarded me with questions. Trying to be polite, I answered the best I could. I was becoming desperate to eat and sit back down with Maria.

Back to the table, the English woman took it upon herself to join us, talking and pontificating. Her main complaint was about the Chilean government and how she knew how to rectify the abuses. It was a subject I knew nothing about and couldn't care less about. I sat stoically eating, nodding my head now and again, wishing she'd shut up so I could get on with Maria. Maria quietly took it in, allowing Clare to express herself.

Henny came over to the table and whispered something into Clare's ear.

Clare responded, "Yes, Darling. I'll be right there."

No sooner had Henny left than Clare stood and picked up her plate,

"Excuse me. I must help Henny. Nice meeting you, Tony."

"Likewise." I answered, glad she was gone.

Maria smiled at me, "Clare's a good person, but sometimes she goes on a bit."

"It looks like Henny knows her job."

"She does." Maria laughed, then came to the point. "Is it possible for you to come out to my ranch and spend a couple of days there?"

Struggling to keep up this ruse, my emotions took over. I had to get a hold of myself. She looked at me when she asked the question. I didn't answer right away. She looked down at her plate and took another bite. God, she was beautiful, so mesmerizing, enchanting.

Our eyes met again. I was at a loss for words, not wanting to carry the burden of following through with the game. I tried to be honest with myself, fascinated by the whole scenario, where I was, and whom I was with. Maria struck my heart. My mind was in a fog.

I leaned back in the chair, brought my hands to my forehead, raised my sight above her head, and then looked back into her eyes, "Yes."

A split second later, I caught myself and blurted out, "But..."

The "but" surprised her as she stiffened, "But what?"

"Before I come, I have to make arrangements."

"Oh, sure, of course."

"I'll tell you what. I need a day or so. You have a phone at the ranch?"

"Yes."

"Let me get your number and as soon as I'm clear, I'll give you a call. How does that sound?"

"Sounds wonderful."

Inner desperation reminded me to mingle with the crowd a bit. I must not act like a love-sick puppy.

"Would you like more paella?" she asked.

"I would."

The party lasted another couple of hours, with music, dancing and eating. I stood with Alec and Maria, discussing the wonders of Ricardo's place and how he had done it all. Maria wandered off with others occasionally, but always returned to me to talk and joke. I wondered if she had the same feeling I did.

Henny came out of the kitchen with an announcement, "Okay, everybody, time to leave!"

I went out with them, escorting Maria to her Land Rover. She turned and hugged me, kissing me on the cheek. Hesitating to uncouple, she looked at me and said, "I look forward to seeing you."

"I'll be in touch," I answered, then kissed her forehead.

She got in, and they made a U-turn as the engines started up. I stood in the street and watched them go. The caravan disappeared around the first bend, and I thought, "WOW!" Standing mesmerized, I turned back toward Ricardo's, and Alec stood on the porch wearing a broad smile.

He put his thumbs in the air, "Come on in for a night cap."

The alcohol dulled my thinking, but one thing I knew for sure was that I was star-struck and wasn't prepared for it. Alec mixed a drink, thanking me for working it out so I could stay over. In my inebriated state, I knew I was in trouble.

CHAPTER 28

The mission was to steal a recipe from a girl I'd fallen in love with. Now, I wanted the girl, not the recipe.

Without the excuse of collecting blood and saliva samples for her llama herd, I was just another guy romantically pursuing her. She had probably been through that a thousand times in her lifetime.

Maria gave no indication she had somebody in her life. That final embrace as she got in the Land Rover, the kiss on the cheek, her saying, "I'm looking forward to seeing you—" was that about blood samples, or did she have feelings? Then reality hit me like a brick: The only way to find out was to keep going and follow the plan to the end. Otherwise, I'd make a fool of myself.

To that end, it was better not to rush out, seeming too anxious. So, before I turned in for the night, having a nightcap with Alec, I told him I had someplace to go and would return in a couple of days.

I had yet to check in with a professor Dr. Wasson worked with at Santiago University. Therefore, it was best to return to Coya and call Ron's friend to validate the alibi. After breakfast, a taxi was waiting for me to return to Coya.

The cab driver stopped at Hotel Parron, which was on the upper side of town, toward the mountains. It was a block building painted burnt orange, with an extended entry leading to a well-manicured lawn and garden area in the front.

Nobody was behind the reception counter, and I hit the bell for service twice.

A wall separated the foyer from a small bar, and the restaurant in the back had four tables. An older gentleman emerged from the restaurant and went behind the counter.

In Spanish, he asked, "How can I help you?"

"Do you have a room available?"

In English, the man answered, "Yes, how many days?"

"One or two."

"That's not a problem. Where are you from?"

"The United States."

After he dealt with the passport, he completed my reservation and handed me the key to room 12, which was up the stairs and to the left.

"One more thing." I asked. "I need to use the telephone."

He pointed across the room to the phone booth.

"Is it possible to call the United States?"

"Dial 01 and wait for the operator."

The room was simple, with a single bed. When I opened the curtains, I saw the town of Coya below.

I needed to call Janet, but it was still early there. She would be at home, and I could call her collect.

I dialed 01, and the operator came on the line. She spoke English, which made the process more manageable.

After three rings, Janet picked it up.

"Hello?" she answered.

"Hey Janet," I blurted out, forgetting the operator needed to get permission for the collect call.

The operator interrupted. "Will you accept a collect call from Tony Taylor?"

"Yes, of course. Put him on."

"Tony. Where are you?"

"I'm in Coya. It's fifteen miles down the road from Ricardo's place."

"How's it going? Are you doing all right?"

"I'm doing well, I came back to Coya after spending two days at Ricardo's. Unbelievably, I met Maria, and she wants me to come to her ranch and look at her llamas."

"You're kidding! How did that happen?"

"I went to the bar at Ricardo's and befriended the bartender and told him what I was doing."

"You didn't tell him everything!"

"No, no, of course not. Then he suggested I meet Maria."

"That's incredible!"

"I know! He arranged the meeting and after a big party Maria asked me to come to her ranch."

"Unbelievable! Why aren't you there now?"

"I didn't want to seem anxious, so I came here to contact Ron's friends in Santiago. I wanted to make sure they'd validate my story in case anybody investigated. I didn't realize things would happen so fast."

"I can't wait to tell Brian. What did you think of Maria?"

"She is everything everybody said about her."

"You're taken by her."

"I'm looking forward to going to her ranch. I'll leave it at that."

"Don't forget the reason you're there."

"I know. I won't be able to contact you until this goes one way or the other, and I have no idea how long it will take."

I hung up the phone, perplexed and dishonest. Although I was trying to play the game, my feelings for Maria were getting in the way. I felt caught in an emotional quagmire, miles from home and in uncharted territory.

My next call was to the Animal Husbandry Department at Santiago University. I contacted Professor Alfonso Herrera. Ron Wasson had contacted Dr. Herrera to let him know I would contact him about this mission. Herrera wanted me to visit the University when the mission was completed to discuss the findings. My story was solid.

During the rest of the day, I walked around Coya. The confluence of the Coya and Cachapoal Rivers divided the town into four quadrants, so to kill time, I decided to check out each section.

The hotel was in the northeast section, which included the main shopping area. On the side of the same hill, stood a large white Catholic church. Walking to the town plaza, I checked my watch every four or five minutes until it drove me crazy. Finally, I took it off and put it in my pocket so I wouldn't have easy access.

Crossing the bridge over the Coya River, I admired the merging rivers below. As I looked down at the river, a white British Land Rover passed me like the ones Maria had brought to Ricardo's. Out of the corner of my eye, I recognized the two French guys from the entourage in the front seats.

My mind raced. All I needed was for Maria or one of her groups to notice me lollygagging around Coya in the middle of the day when I was supposed to be out on assignment. I picked up my step. Getting back to the hotel and staying out of sight would be better. Fears of blowing my cover racked my brain.

I hurried along the street towards the shopping area. Ahead was the Land Rover parked in front of the food market. Nearing the market, one of the Frenchies came out of the store carrying bags and looked my way. Not wanting to be caught outside, I ducked into the store to my right. I thought how stupid I was for being out in the open.

I waited for them to leave; I looked around and noticed this was a small seafood market.

A seafood market here in the middle of Coya? I pondered. How far were they from the ocean to have so many species of fish iced on metal trays? One tray looked like salmon. Do they have salmon down here? On the other side were iced trays of crab, shrimp, and clams; the last was oysters. Oysters! How strange to find oysters in Coya!

This treasure trove of seafood products calmed me down. If things turned out how I hoped they would, this little shop might be the key to the big prize.

When I looked out the window, the Land Rover was gone. I made a quick exit and hurried up the street to the hotel. I went directly to the bar and ordered straight bourbon. I downed it in two gulps and ordered another.

I started the second bourbon, and a commotion came from the lobby. Two English-speaking men with a Texas accent laughed as they carried their luggage into the bar, looking for a drink.

I turned to the men; we acknowledged each other with a nod. They wore Levi's, cowboy boots, long-sleeved western shirts, and cowboy hats. Stepping up to the bar, they ordered Cervezas Colonos.

As the bartender poured their drinks, I broke the ice by saying, "It looks like you guys have been here before."

Surprised to hear an American accent, the taller of the two responded, "We have." Sticking out his hand to shake, "I'm Tom Wade and this is Dave Martin."

I stood and shook their hands, "I'm Tony Taylor. Don't tell me you're from Texas."

"How can you tell?" Tom laughed.

"I spent some time near Texas in the Army."

Before they answered, the bartender handed them their beer. Taking a hardy drink, they finished off half the glass. Putting his glass on the bar, Tom wiped his mouth and said, "Army, probably Fort Bliss?"

"Fort Sill, Oklahoma, artillery training."

"Dave and I were in the Marines together. We made it through the Pacific war."

"Two beers for my friends," I told the bartender.

They thanked me for the beers and sat at one of the tables, "Come and join us."

With my bourbon, I sat down, "What are two Texans doing in Coya Chile?"

"Fishing." Tom answered.

"Fishing! What kind of fishing?"

"Steelhead."

"Steelhead fishing! You've got to be kidding me."

"Some of the best steelhead fishing is right here."

"I never would have thought that."

"Two years ago, Dave caught a thirty-five pounder."

"Thirty-five pounds, I didn't know they even got that big."

"Get bigger than that. There are fifty pounders in these waters."

"Are there salmon here?"

"No salmon, but you can hardly tell the difference in the meat, same color, texture and everything."

"Taste the same?"

"I'd say so."

I noticed their gear piled on the lobby floor. Each had a large leather bag with four tubes strapped to them.

"Are those rods strapped to your bags?"

"Yep, fly rods. We only fly fish. When you catch a large steelhead on a fly line you really have something."

I thought of the oyster wrap; I could pull it off using a fresh steelhead.

Then I asked, "Where do you go?"

"We start out in the Coya River and fish it for a day or so and then work our way around to the Cachapoal. That's what makes this place so unique, we have two rivers to work."

"Which is the best?"

"It depends. You never know. Dave caught that thirty-five pounder up the Cachapoal."

"Are you two the only ones who know this?"

"No. We're the first. It's the start of the steelhead season. In a week or two this place will be crawling with anglers."

"When do you start fishing?"

"First thing in the morning."

We bought more rounds of drinks and ordered dinner, getting to know each other. The cowboys were curious why I was there. They thought my research on llamas and hoof-and-mouth disease was interesting because they ran small cattle ranches in Texas.

As the evening wore on, Tom asked if I'd like to join them in the morning. He offered me one of his poles to see how I liked it.

I needed to kill time. I could add fly fishing in Chile to my resume, which would be more impressive. They set a time to meet back in the restaurant at five a.m. for breakfast and get out at first light. We stuck around for a nightcap, which turned into three more rounds before retiring.

CHAPTER 29

A voice came from the hallway. "Desyunos, Señor." I hurried to relieve myself in the bathroom from last night's too many bourbons. My head felt like a marshmallow.

Tom and Dave sat at one of the tables sipping hot coffee. "Good morning," laughed Tom. "You're still alive?"

The table had three plates, silverware, a small glass of orange juice, a glass of water, and hot coffee with a plate of toast and cheese.

"Alive, but barely."

Taking a drink of coffee, it burnt my mouth, "Whew… hot!"

Tom and Dave looked amused, watching me clear the cobwebs in my brain.

"How did you sleep?" Tom laughed again.

"Hardly remember going to bed."

"You remember we helped you up the stairs?"

"I think I do, but that's about it."

"Are you going to be able to make it?"

"I'll make it. I just need food in my gut."

The waiter brought three plates containing a large omelet, sausage, and bacon and placed them in front of us.

While eating my omelet, I asked, "What do I need to bring?"

"Do you have waders?"

"The only shoes I have are the ones I'm wearing."

"I have an extra set of rubber boots you can wear. When we get down to the river, I'll put on my waders, and you can use my boots," said Tom.

"That's generous of you. You know I don't have any fishing gear either."

"We figured that. We both have extra rods and reels. We'll set you up."

"I can't thank you enough. I don't know how to repay you."

"You can buy dinner tonight. How's that?"

I went to my room to get my pack. When I got back, Tom and Dave were wearing packs, holding fishing gear, and standing by the door. Tom held a pair of boots.

"What size do you wear?"

"A size nine."

"These are tens. Might be a bit sloppy, but they'll work."

The waiter brought us each a bag of lunch. After leaving the hotel, we went to the Coya River Bridge.

I thought about Maria and how this would fit into the plan. The adventure was going so well that I felt like an actor in a play waiting for it to blow up in my face.

We climbed down the bank to the river in the dark at the bridge. I reminded them I was a novice and wanted to watch before casting my line. We planned to work up the river half a mile past the town limits. Tom and Dave laid their gear on the riverbank and opened their packs. Tom pulled out rolled-up waders. It started to get light when they took off their footwear, climbed into the waders, and me into borrowed rubber boots.

Tom opened a tube, removed three sections of his fly rods, and slid one section into the other. He then removed a fly reel from his packs and attached it to the rod. He strung the line through the guides and pulled it out six feet from the end.

A lighter fishing line was used as a leader, and a special knot attached to the heavier line. The fishing vests contained small metal tins. Tom opened one tin and picked out a hook dressed like an insect.

"Did you make those flies?" I asked.

"We make all our flies. That's the fun of it."

"It's a real art, then."

They laughed. "You can say that, especially when you hook into a fifteen pounder."

Tom tied a fly to the end of his leader and attached the hook on the first guide of the rod. He reeled in the line tight and set it on a rock. Meanwhile, Dave finished his setup and walked to the river.

Tom set up a rod for me and showed me how to tie the fly to the leader. He handed me the rod and a tin full of flies.

"This tin is in case you lose your fly," he cautioned.

Dave cast his line and let it drift down the shallow rocky river bottom. We moved forty yards up the river.

"You said you've done this before, so I'll watch a second to check out your technique."

With each cast, I fed out more line. It was important to use a fluid motion, allowing the line and hook to come forward so the fly would travel to the end of the line and leader.

The first couple of times, I didn't do so well. After a couple of tips from Tom, I got the hang of it and allowed the fly to drift forty feet down the current.

"You're doing okay. Have fun," Tom said.

He turned upriver and yelled, "Hey, look at that!"

Dave unhooked a three-pounder and released it into the river—the day's first fish in less than fifteen minutes. I got excited watching Dave, thinking, "This is going to be a good day."

I cast with no luck. Dave moved up my way, calling out, "After ten or fifteen casts, if you don't get a strike, move up the river."

"Thanks," I acknowledged, watching Dave head upstream.

I started upriver in time to see Tom hook a fish.

It was a nice one. His pole bent and jerked. The fish broke the surface and flew three feet in the air. He played the fish like a pro and slowly brought the line in until it was near. The fish played out. He bent down and picked it up by the lower lip. It was a nice fish, bigger than Dave's fish.

Retrieving the hook, he gently released the fish back into the river.

As the morning progressed, we worked our way up the Coya River. Tom and Dave caught fish everywhere they stopped, but I had yet to get a bite. Frustrated, but determined, I remained focused on Maria and my mission.

We stopped to take a break and ate our snacks. Tom sympathized with me.

"Don't worry about it. We have days like this. We might need to change the fly."

He picked one out, "This one will work better. The problem is the fly gets saturated and sinks rather than floats on top."

He clipped off the old fly with fingernail clippers and tied on the new one. I was anxious to try out this new fly.

After the snack, Tom pointed to the river and said, "Try over there, and keep your fly in the air to dry it out."

I cast as they watched. In two seconds, I got a strike, and it was a big one.

Tom and Dave jumped up and rushed to me, giving instructions. "Don't force it; keep the line taut."

The pole bent like a candy cane. I worked the line with my left hand.

"Play him out. Let him run if he wants to. It looks like you have a nice one," said Tom.

The fish broke the water and jumped three feet in the air.

Dave yelled, "That's a good ten, twelve-pound fish!"

"Work him in slowly, but give him room," Tom instructed.

When the fish relaxed a little, I reeled in line. When he started to run, I eased up and gave him room. Tenderly, I worked the fish to the shore until it lay at my feet.

I looked at it with pride, removed the hook, and lifted it by the lower lip. We admired it, and then I eased the fish into the water to allow it to work its gills for fresh oxygen. As it slowly swam away, Tom and Dave held out their hands to congratulate me on my first catch—a big Chilean Steelhead.

We moved up and down the river. I caught four more, but none bigger than the first one. Dave and Tom caught more fish, but I lost count.

When the fishing slowed, Tom said, "We'll wrap it up for now and head back to the hotel. Later in the evening, things will pick up again.

We'll try the Cachapoal this evening."

On the way back, my thoughts centered on Maria. I needed to get fishing gear. Her ranch bordered the Cachapoal River. Knowing where to get oysters, I knew that just one of these fat steelheads could suffice for salmon, and I could treat her to an oyster wrap.

"Thanks for letting me tag along." I said.

"No problem. We're glad you caught that twelve pounder."

"It was exciting. You have me hooked on fly fishing."

"It doesn't take much after experiencing a strike like the one you had."

"While I'm down here, I figure I should take advantage of it, which begs the question, where can I find fishing gear?"

"There is Julio's in Rancagua. He has everything you'll need: fly rods and reels."

"What about flies? I never tied flies before."

"He has pre-tied flies by the hundreds and can help you pick out the best ones for these rivers."

"Do you want to go out with us again this evening?" Tom asked.

"I'd better get into Julio's this afternoon. I have an appointment tomorrow I can't miss."

Back at the hotel, it was noon. The clerk informed me that bus #3 ran to Rancagua every hour. I could be back at the hotel by dinner time. Before I left, I went to the phone booth and dialed Maria's number. Henny picked it up. I recognized her voice.

"Hello, Henny. I'm Tony Taylor, the guy you met at Ricardo's the other night."

"Sure Tony. How are you?"

"I'm fine, thank you. Is Maria anywhere around?"

"She is out in the orchard, but she told me if you called to ask when you might be coming?"

"I can come tomorrow, if that's all right."

"That would be great. A driver will pick you up. Where and what time to meet you."

"Would the market in Coya at 9 a.m. be too difficult?"

"Of course not. We go there all the time. The driver will come in a white Land Rover."

"I'll look out for him. See you tomorrow?"

"I'll tell Maria. She'll be very happy. Bye for now."

Those last words made my heart race. Maria would be pleased to see me, so I hung up and left the hotel for the bus stop, where I would wait for Bus #3.

I got back to the hotel early in the evening, geared up for fly fishing.

I was starting on my second drink when Tom and Dave came in, fresh from the river. I went to greet them, wearing my vest and carrying my bag.

"Well look at this!" said Tom as we greeted each other. "Julio had what you needed."

"He did. He has a wide selection."

"Where are you going to start fishing?" Tom asked. "You can go out with us again tomorrow."

"I'd love to, but I have to go to a ranch tomorrow and check on livestock."

Suddenly, his demeanor changed and became authoritative when he asked, "Would it be Maria Hollmann's place?"

Caught off guard by this new attitude, "It is. How did you figure that?"

"We've run into her a couple of times. She's very pretty and spends time with interesting people. How long are you going to stay up there? Enough time to fish I suppose?"

Tom's continual probing made me feel uncomfortable like there was more to these questions than was apparent.

"Don't know for sure. I only know they are sending a driver to pick me up tomorrow at nine."

"How well do you know Maria?" asked Tom.

"Not that well. I met her the night before last at Ricardo's. Why do you ask?"

"Just curious. Her father worked for the government as a forester. He was a German Nazi. They're down here, still on the run."

I found it strange Tom was so interested when he brought up another subject.

"The communists are trying to make inroads into South America. This will bring a crisis, and bloodshed. The old guards don't want to give up power, and they are willing to do whatever they need to stay in power."

"I never thought much about it. I'm not up on the politics of South America."

"Sometimes it gets deadly," Tom continued, "Dave and I would like to stay in touch with you to see how the fishing is upriver at Maria's ranch. You say you don't know how long you'll be there?"

"Not for sure."

"We'll be around. Hopefully, we can catch up before you leave the area."

Tired of this grilling, I answered, "I can't make plans, I have several commitments that are going to be pressing."

"Of course, but we'll be looking out for you."

I was plagued by thoughts of this conversation. What did Tom mean when he said they would be looking out for me?

CHAPTER 30

I got out early and figured I'd have to wait, but when I got to the market, the Land Rover was waiting, with no one around. Inside the store, the Frenchman was buying a pack of cigarettes. My thought was, *Great, the Frenchman. What will we talk about for the twenty-minute ride to Maria's?*

When the Frenchman emerged, I leaned against the front fender. He opened his pack of cigarettes, glanced at me, and unceremoniously nodded.

I remembered his name as François. A thin, six-foot-tall man, he wore all black. His long, pointy nose and protruding cheekbones shaded his sunken cheeks. His greased hair combed straight back, exposed a high forehead.

In a strong French accent, with no formal greeting, "Are you ready, Monsieur?"

I tossed my luggage in the back, sat down, and waited for him to fish out a cigarette. He lit it on his way to the driver's door, slid into the seat, and reached for the keys. He took a big drag and exhaled, filling the cab with smoke. With a cigarette hanging from his lips, he started the engine.

When we reached the outskirts of Coya, I felt I should start a conversation, "Where in France are you from?"

With a smirk, he looked at me, "What makes you think I come from France?"

Was he joking or being a smartass?

"Because you speak with a French accent."

"That is true. But you know they speak French in Belgium and Switzerland, also."

"Are you saying you're from Belgium?"

He slightly rolled down the window to let out the smoke, "My family lives in Marseilles,"

I hoped this would end in twenty minutes. I found it hard to like this Frenchman.

"I hear there are some beautiful women in Marseilles."

"You like women?"

"I do. You don't like them?"

"I like the women, but I prefer the young boys. You never tried the young boys?" he asked.

"Can't say I have."

"Even in the Army you never tried the young boys?"

"Even in the Army I never tried the young boys."

"What a shame, those young boys have gone to waste."

"It's too bad you never joined the Army, François. Think about it. You could have taken a shower every night with fifty naked young studs."

He jerked his head around and stared at me. Eyes on the road, he threw out his cigarette butt and began to laugh. "Tony, you are a funny man!"

"That's what I've been told."

The next few moments, driving in silence, I tried again.

"What's a Frenchman doing here in Chile?"

"What am I doing in Chile?" he paused. "I'm a socialist, and there is a strong socialist movement here. I want to see how it goes."

"A socialist, you mean a communist?"

"You can say a communist."

"I hear this is not a safe place for communists down here."

"It depends on who you know."

"Who do you know that will keep you safe?" I chuckled.

"Maria."

"Maria! What's her take on what's happening?"

"Mister Tony, you have to ask her that question."

After a few minutes, François asked, "Where are you from, Mister

Tony?"

"San Francisco. You ever been there?"

"I've never been to the United States, but I know people from there, even San Francisco."

"Who do you know?"

"A woman named Janet."

I sat back momentarily, thinking this guy couldn't know Janet.

"Maybe you know her?" he asked.

"There are a lot of women in San Francisco named Janet."

"That's true, but this woman is an art dealer and owns art galleries. Have you heard of her?"

I stared out the window and told a lie. "I don't know any Janet who's an art dealer."

"Such a pity, she is a very nice femme."

We traveled up the road until we took a left turn up a gravel lane. A curved sign had *Mariposa* written on it—an orchard on the right and a well-manicured lawn on the left. A large white ranch house with a red terracotta tiled roof appeared.

"We are here," announced the Frenchman, driving to the house entrance.

The large porch had an arched ten-foot-high opening, flanked with smaller openings the same height—large terracotta flower pots planted with brightly colored flowers. The double-recessed wooden entry door swung on black metal hinges.

Henny bounded forward as I got out of the car.

She reached out her hand, "Welcome to the Mariposa."

"Thank you. What a beautiful place," I answered.

I looked at the Frenchman, "Thanks for the ride."

"No problem. I needed cigarettes, anyway."

Henny bent to take the bag, "Come. Let me take you to your room."

I beat her to the bags, "I can get those. They might be too heavy for you."

Left of the entryway was a series of six rooms. She led me through an arch into the covered passageway beyond the main house. She opened the first door and motioned for me to enter first.

The room was spacious, with terracotta floor tiles throughout. On the back wall was a window over a double bed with a carved wooden headboard, the same design I'd seen at Ricardo's.

Henny opened the bathroom door. "Here is your bathroom, which you share with the next room. Fortunately, nobody is in there, so you have it to yourself." She stepped aside to allow me to look.

"I hope you'll be comfortable here."

"Very cozy. I'll be more than fine."

"Do you know how long you will be staying? We hope it's more than a day or two. Maria is excited to have you."

"I don't know for sure. We'll see what happens. I don't have too long."

While Henny showed me my room, I wondered where Maria and her other guests were. This introduction to the grounds was part of some protocol.

"You can leave your things here. Come, I'll show you around the rest of the house."

Leaving the room, I asked, "Where is everybody?"

"They're around. The guests sleep in quite late." She looked at her watch, "Maria should be here anytime. She rides her horse every morning to check her animals in the field."

"She rides, does she?"

Henny stopped at the main front door and looked at me, "She is an excellent equestrian, one of the loves of her life. Do you ride?"

"I was practically born on a horse. It was my mother's passion, and she made sure my brother and I were acquainted with the ways of a horse."

"Maria will be glad to hear that."

Opening the large wooden door, she ushered me in.

The foyer had white walls and a terracotta floor. A chandelier hung from the open-beam cathedral ceiling. Centered in the main room was an open brick fire pit with a cone-shaped flue. Four large red leather couches, with glass end tables between them, surrounded the pit. A large wooden dining table with twelve matching chairs sat in the rear of the room. Glass doors made up half of the back wall. They opened to a covered porch facing the mountains in the distance.

Henny explained how Maria's father designed and built this grand house and lived here with Maria before he died. I was impressed as I imagined the history of the ranch.

"How long ago did Maria's father build this place?"

"He came here during the war and obtained the property. He started construction soon after that."

"That means this house is almost twenty years old."

"I think so. But Maria can answer those questions for you better than I can. Let me show you the kitchen."

In the kitchen, the English woman, Clare, sat with open cookbooks, writing at a desk against the back wall.

Clare jumped up, "Tony, what a delight it is to see you, Darling." She rushed over to hug me and kiss my right cheek. "We've been waiting for your arrival. Come sit down and I'll heat the kettle. Looks like you're dying for a cup of tea."

Clare didn't give me a chance to respond as she went to a large oil-burning Aga stove, took a tea kettle to the other side of the kitchen to a large porcelain sink, and pumped the handle while she bombarded me with questions I could not answer.

I glanced around, admiring this expansive utilitarian kitchen. It looked like it was out of the nineteen-thirties.

Henny asked, "Clare, are you sure he wants a cup of tea?"

"Of course, he wants a cup of tea. Don't you, Darling?" more of a statement than a question.

I realized I had no way out of it, "A cup of tea would be fine."

"You see, Cherub, Clare knows what a man needs. I made a fresh plate of scones this morning. Henny, put chairs around the table, and we'll try them."

She placed the kettle on the stove, took a metal cover off a plate piled with scones, and placed them on the prep table in the middle of the kitchen. A shelf under the table was stacked with pots and pans of assorted sizes and shapes.

This kitchen was built for serious cooking. A large food pantry filled with various gourmet food items stood in one corner. One wall of the larder held shelves with spice jars. Next to the pantry was a large built-in refrigerator. I couldn't tell what was in there, but I was sure it was well stocked.

The kettle's water began to boil. Clare lifted the lid and added three large tablespoons of tea. Then she went into the pantry and came out with two jars. She asked, "Strawberry or marmalade?"

I thought for a moment, "Marmalade."

She looked at Henny, "I know you like strawberry."

Clare brought over both jars and placed them on the table. Then, she brought out a covered dish of fresh homemade butter and put three small plates and teacups around the table.

"Please sit down, both of you," she implored, filling the teacups.

"Tony, Darling, you haven't answered any of my questions," Clare chided.

"I'm sorry, Clare, I was taken in by this incredible kitchen."

"It is perfect, isn't it?"

"I'd say so."

"You do know that Maria, besides running the ranch and her animals, is a world-renowned culinary artist?"

She placed a scone on each plate and opened the marmalade and strawberry jars.

Once again, feeling squeamish, I lied and said, "No, I didn't know that."

"Of course she is. That's why I'm here to help her and keep things organized in the kitchen."

"Sounds like she's a woman of many talents."

"That she is, as you will find out."

"I'm sure I will."

"How long do you plan to stay with us? Maria thinks you are in big demand."

"I have a lot to do in a short time, no more than a day or two."

How would I justify staying longer if the situation demanded it and keeping up the ruse? I opened the scone, applied a good helping of marmalade, and took the first bite. My mouth was full of scone. The kitchen door opened, and there stood Maria.

"Tony, it's so nice to see you. Thank you for coming," she said as she hugged me.

I stood, trying to chew and swallow the scone before she got to me. My mouth was too dry to swallow as we embraced. Desperate to swallow, I placed my mouth next to her ear as I held her embrace. She tilted her head back to look at me, realized my dilemma, and laughed.

I stepped back. She allowed me to finish the scone. I put my hand to my mouth and lowered my head to get the last of the scone down my throat.

I looked back at her, "These are really good scones," I said, embarrassed.

Still laughing, she went to the counter and picked up another cup and dish. "Clare knows her scones."

She poured a cup of tea, placed a scone on her dish, brought a chair next to Henny, and sat down.

She looked at me, "How long do we get you for?"

"I have a tight schedule."

"I'm aware of that. I'd like to take you around and show you the ranch as soon as possible."

"I'm looking forward to it."

"The best way to see it is by horseback, do you ride?"

"Like a Comanche chief," I answered as they laughed.

"Great, I'll have Juan saddle up one of the horses and we'll start as soon as possible. Henny, could you go tell Juan to saddle up Chessie for us and we'll get going?"

Henny jumped up, leaving half her scone and tea, "Yes, of course."

Maria stopped her, "Finish your tea first. We're not in that big of a hurry."

"I'll get Juan and finish when I get back."

"You are a sweetheart."

Henny went out the back door to the veranda as I finished the last of my scone.

Clare said, "That will be lovely, and when you get back, we'll have pheasant for dinner. I have two hanging in the pantry. Jorge brought me them yesterday. You do like pheasant don't you, Tony?"

"One of my favorites," stretching the truth.

"Clare does wonders with pheasant."

Maria continued, "I want to take you out to the barn, and show you my sick little animals. Then I'll show you around."

"Sounds great. How many llamas do you have?"

"At last count we had three hundred, forty head of cattle, and five milking Guernsey cows."

"Don't forget the eight horses," Clare broke in.

"Yes, Clare, eight horses."

"Are they Paso Fino?" I asked.

"They are. You know your horses, I see."

"Only by name. I hear they're a tough breed, bred especially for this area."

"That's right, you'll be on one of my favorites as soon as Juan brings them up. I assume you've had horses?"

"My mom taught my brother and me to ride as soon as we were old enough to walk."

"That's interesting. What breed did you have?"

"She was a quarter horse, a lively little thing of about fourteen hands."

"What was her name?"

"Pickle."

Maria giggled, "That's a cute name, how did you come by that?"

"When I was a kid, I loved sweet pickles, so I named her Pickle."

Clare laughed with Maria, trying to control herself, as I drank the last of my tea.

Henny came in and announced Juan was on his way.

"Oh good," said Maria. "Come follow me."

Clare and Henny watched us leave. "Have a good ride!" Clare shouted. "Thanks for the tea and scone. They were great."

CHAPTER 31

I followed Maria to the veranda. The view of the foothills leading up to the snowcapped Andes was breathtaking.

"Nice view you have here."

"I feel so fortunate. It is a dream come true."

"That's understandable."

Juan came up on one of the horses, the other in tow.

"Juan is on Bandolero and Chessie is behind. She is a great horse. I'm sure you'll love her."

"I'm sure I will."

Juan stopped short, jumped off the horse, and handed the reins to Maria.

"Thanks, Juan. This is Tony. He'll be here for a couple of days."

"Mucho gusto, Señor Tony."

"Igualmente." I answered.

I didn't hesitate to take the reins. I showed no fear as I put my left foot in the stirrup, grabbed the saddle horn, and hoisted myself up as Maria and Juan looked on. To evaluate how the horse would respond to my lead, I gave her a little kick, turned her to the right, and did a figure eight. There was an instant connection between man and horse, so I halted before them.

"Ready," I said.

Maria and Juan were stunned by my display of horsemanship and were unresponsive until Maria caught herself. "Yes."

She lifted herself atop her horse and took the reins. "Follow me."

She took off at a gallop toward the barn with me in hot pursuit. Halfway to the barn, she slowed to a gait to allow me to catch up.

"Very impressive. You do know how to ride."

"My mother had me on a horse almost before I could walk."

"Do you like this gait of the Paso Fino?"

"It's like riding on a carousel. This is what you were talking about. I could get used to this."

"I'm so glad you could find time to come. I'm hoping you can stay long enough to get the full Chilean experience."

At the barn, Maria dismounted and tied Bandolero to a hitching post.

"Come with me," she beckoned as I dismounted.

Inside the barn, skylights on the roof gave abundant light. She took hold of my hand and led me in. The feel of her hand in mine caused my blood to rush with excitement.

Both sides had stalls spread with fresh straw for the llamas. She let go of my hand, opened the first gate, and bent over, gently stroking the animal.

"These are my sick babies."

I opened the mouth and inspected for disease around its lips. I took hold of the top of the right leg and worked my way down to examine the underside of the nails.

There was a small amount of pus around the nails as Maria watched intently.

I looked at Maria, "You have a problem here."

"I hope you have a solution."

"I can take blood and saliva samples and send them into the lab to see where we go from here."

"How long will it take?"

"It won't take long to get the samples, but I must get them to the lab in Santiago for results. From there we'll be able to tell if Doctor Wasson's antiviral will work on this strain."

"We have hope then?"

"Let me check out a few more animals and I'll get my sample kit."

The next animal had the same symptoms.

Looking toward the sink by the barn door, I said, "I need to wash my hands."

I turned on the tap and scrubbed my hands with the bar of soap provided. After drying my hands, I turned to find Maria's face inches from mine. She didn't step back but moved closer to my lips. I didn't resist as our lips compressed together.

Slightly opening her mouth, she allowed my tongue to enter and explore hers. Explosions of emotions and desire went off in my body as I pulled her into my arms, and we held each other in a tight embrace, lips, and tongues ever searching. I didn't want it to end.

Suddenly, I bolted with a shocking thought: *This is going too fast. She'll see through me if I don't follow through with the mission.*

I broke the embrace."I'd better go get my kit and get these samples," I said.

"Ohhh…" she sighed, opening her eyes with a quaint smile. "I'll go with you."

I had to rip myself away to get the kit, even though I wanted to stay in the barn with Maria and finish what we started. With my mind and emotions tangled, I had to keep composure to see this through.

We mounted the horses, turned toward the big house, and took off at a gallop. How could this be happening? I'd only been there an hour when Maria came over to me. How was I going to manage the events needed to get this damn recipe?

I wanted to confess everything and take her in my arms again, but she'd realize I was an imposter. That would turn out harmful and embarrassing, so far away from home, with nowhere to go.

I thought of Janet and how she worked out the plot. She manipulated everything and pushed me into this dilemma. After what happened in the barn, solving the problem of Maria's animals was my only hope.

We dismounted at the house and went to my room. I opened my pack as Maria sat on the bed and intensely watched. Inside my pack were a syringe, three small, stoppered test tubes with needles inside, glass slides wrapped in wax paper, and a small packet of cotton swabs.

I looked at Maria and said, "These needles are sterilized. Once I draw the blood, I'll reseal the tubes to keep them as sterile as possible."

"Looks like you know what you're doing."

"I've done it a few times." Giving her a wink, bringing a smile to her face.

"For the saliva, I take cotton swabs and swipe them around the mouth and under the tongue, then rub the swabs on these glass slides, sealing it by sandwiching two together. We'll need three samples from three animals and label them One, Two, and Three. We must remember which animal is One, Two and Three."

Maria laughed, "I think I can manage that."

While I repacked the kit, Maria leaned over, kissed my forehead, and kissed my lips.

I smiled at her, "We'd better get this done. We need to get these samples to Dr. Herrera's lab in Santiago within three days. I'll have to leave right away and catch the bus to get them there on time."

Maria sat down on the bed, looking confused. I stood up to leave. As I reached for the door, she stared at the wall.

"Wait a moment. Give me a minute to think."

I let go of the door handle and looked at Maria, waiting for her to say something.

"You mean you have to leave as soon as you take the samples?"

"I have to get them to the lab on time before they spoil."

She looked down, "I don't want you to leave right now. You just got here."

She looked at me. I didn't know what to say or how to maneuver through this crisis. I didn't want to leave but couldn't give up the excuse of a busy schedule. If I was going to get good samples, I had to take them to the lab immediately.

Maria stood up, stepped toward me, and grabbed my wrists. "I know you're busy, but can we take the samples tomorrow? I'd love to have you spend the night with us, and Clare has this dinner planned. I didn't realize the urgency of the process."

I had to get control of myself.

I took her hands, sat her on the bed, picked up the backpack, and replaced the kit. "Maria, I'm sorry I lost control and kissed you. I got ahead of myself. I must admit I've become very fond of you in so short a time. But I'm not sure it's the best thing for either of us to get intimate so fast. Our lives are different. Do you mind if we back up and restart?"

She stood, "I'm not sorry. I knew you were special the first time I saw you sitting at the bar. Getting to know you has confirmed my feelings. You are special and the fact you've come all this way to do what you do proves it. I know it's crazy, but I can't help the way I feel about you. Do you mind giving me the liberty to feel about you the way I do? Besides, I know you feel the same about me."

Stunned by her answer, she continued in a quagmire.

"I have an idea about the samples. Why don't we wait until the morning to take them? Then, I can have my driver deliver them to Dr. Herrera tomorrow. We can call him and arrange where to deliver them, and they should be in his hands by late tomorrow night."

"I don't want to burden you with that."

She spoke more firmly, "It's not a burden. We do this all the time. Please say yes. There is so much I want to show you around here. I'm sure you won't be disappointed."

"It's not that I'd be disappointed, of course I wouldn't be, it's that...."

I stopped to gather my thoughts, not knowing what to say next.

She diverted her eyes and lowered her head to give me time to think. Now, a real fear took hold of me. If these feelings for each other were real, I would have nothing to offer Maria. She had the ranch, herds of cattle and llamas, and friends from around the world who traveled days to visit each other. She had Ricardo's and Alec's. She had Chile, her father's legacy, and a passion and mind to keep it going. I had Janet and Brian and a game to steal recipes from people like her. I wanted to grab my knapsack, run back to Santiago, take the next plane to San Francisco, and forget everything.

She raised her head. and I looked down at her. I couldn't resist. My heart melted. "We can do it tomorrow," I answered.

She took the pack out of my hands, threw it on the bed, and took my hand.

"Let's go for a ride, I want to show you something."

CHAPTER 32

She led me through the living room, where Francois and his partner sat, drinking wine and chatting with the Hungarian girl. Maria stopped and asked them in French what they planned to do for the rest of the day.

François answered, "Nous allons à la rivière pour voir si les poissons courent."

She turned to me and said, "They are going to the river to see if the fish have arrived."

"By fish, you mean steelhead?"

"You know about steelhead?"

"I love steelhead fishing."

"That's interesting. You'll have a chance to catch one."

"I hope so. I have a great steelhead recipe."

"That's more interesting. Hopefully, you'll be here long enough for us to try it out."

François and I exchanged a passing glance as I entered the kitchen. Clare had the pheasant plucked and laid out on the cutting board, busily mixing the stuffing in a large porcelain bowl. Looking at them, she said, "Has Doctor Tony figured out the problem with the llama?"

"We're going to take samples in the morning and ship them off to Santiago for analysis."

"Ship them off?"

"I'll have Juan drive them to the university as soon as we get them. We worked it out so Tony can stay with us for a couple of days."

"Oh splendid, how fun!"

"We're going out for a ride; I want to show him the ranch."

"Be careful. I don't want him to miss these pheasants. They will be extra scrumptious just for him."

"No worries. I'll bring him back in one piece."

Maria went to the larder, "Clare, where is that macramé shoulder bag? I want to take snacks."

"Yes, Dear. I believe it's hanging on the back porch."

Maria hurried to the porch door and took the bag off the hook. On the way to the larder, she stopped to check out the stuffing, pinching off a taste.

"That's going to be good, Clare."

"I think so," Clare responded.

Maria took another pinch and reached across the counter, offering it to me. I leaned over the counter as she placed it in my mouth, allowing her fingers to linger on my lips. Not missing a beat, Clare noticed out of the corner of her eye and turned her head, amused.

From the larder, Maria took a hunk of cheese and salami. "Great stuffing, Clare. It should make those birds stand up."

"What's in it?" I asked.

"I don't like giving up my secrets, but for you, it's long grain rice with apricots plus lots of garlic and other delicacies. Do you spend time in the kitchen?" Clare asked.

"Cooking is one of my hobbies. I'm looking forward to tasting the finished product."

Maria put a bottle of wine, two small glasses, and a paring knife into her bag. She thrust the bag over her head to rest on her back. She took another pinch of stuffing and gazed at me tenderly, "You are full of surprises!"

She headed for the door, "We're off. Be back before dinner."

"Give him a good tour. I'm sure he'll be impressed."

We mounted the horses. Maria headed for the apple orchard, where her cattle were lazily grazing. She reached from her horse and picked four apples off a tree.

"These are Braeburn apples my father planted twenty years ago. They're so sweet. I love to pick them and eat them fresh from the tree."

She handed one to me and put two in her bag, "Take a bite."

We rode out of the orchard, enjoying the apples that cracked with every bite. "You like them?"

"Very crisp, a bit tart."

"You know what they say, 'Apple without cheese is like a kiss without a squeeze.'"

"That's what my mother says."

"Your mother is a wise woman, must know her apples."

"She is and knows her cheese. Where to next?"

"I'm going to surprise you."

"You lead; I'll follow."

She kicked her horse, and at a gallop, we came to a trail leading up the hill. The trail was narrow enough to require us to ride single-file with Maria in the lead. After a short distance, a cut dropped down into a ravine with a small stream flanked by scrub trees on either side. Maria paused so I could see a waterfall splashing into a manufactured swimming hole.

I thought we'd arrived, but she resumed the trek, past the waterfall for a hundred meters, crossed the creek, still ascending. She stopped at a rocky bank and dismounted next to a planted post.

She tied off her horse, "We have to walk from here."

I dismounted, tied the horse to the post, and scrambled to catch up. She climbed a well-worn bank where people had gone before. I lost sight of her when she rounded a large rock. As I rounded the rock, I spotted her fifteen feet above as she stepped out onto the ledge.

"You're here. Keep to the right."

I climbed the last bit and stood winded. She sat on a flat rock next to a steaming pool of water and took the bag off her shoulder. Breathless, I was in awe. There was every natural wonder that humans could desire.

She opened the bottle, "Would you like a glass of wine?"

I sat beside her as she poured the red wine into the glass, "That would be nice."

She cut a slice of apple and cheese and handed it to me, reminding me, "Apple without cheese...."

She cut one for herself, and she moved closer, our hips and thighs touching. After eating the apple and cheese in two bites, I finished it off with the wine. She cut more and handed it to me, this time with a slice of salami. She took my glass and topped it off.

"How did you find this place?"

"I didn't. My father did. He heard about this hot spring and came to see it when he was working in this area. He liked it so much he bought this hill and the property for the ranch."

"How did he hear about it?"

"Ricardo."

"Ricardo. Your father knew Ricardo?"

"He used to collaborate with my father in forestry."

"Now it comes together. You and Ricardo's family go far back."

"Way back before I was born. I grew up with Ricardo's family, Manuela and Alec and the rest."

"You're one big extended family."

"We are."

She handed me another slice of apple and cheese.

"Does this hot spring get used much?"

"Everyone who comes to visit comes here at least once. But as you can tell, it's not easy to get to."

"You got that right."

"I like to come here alone to get away from everything and soak and empty my mind."

"Running your operation takes a lot of effort."

"It does, but I love it and wouldn't change it for the world."

She refilled my glass.

"You get a lot of visitors."

"That's the fun part. Could you do me a favor and pull my boots off?"

When I saw the hot spring, I knew what she had in mind. I was no fool. But I couldn't reconcile why she was enamored with me when she had so many friends. She must have male suitors. But on the other hand, I thought, "Why not?" If she wanted to do this, I'd roll with it.

She extended her leg; I pulled off the right boot and left. Then, she pulled her socks off.

She stood in front of me, inches apart, not backing away. She reached down, undoing her belt and trousers, and pushed them down over her hips, allowing them to fall to the ground. I couldn't help but look. Her legs were tan, shapely, and firm. She wore black silk panties, giving me a show I couldn't help taking in.

She stepped out of her pants, lost her balance, and giggled as I took her arms to steady her. I released her arms; she didn't hesitate to lift the sweater and shirt over her head, exposing a matching black silk see-through bra. She laid her sweater and shirt on the rock, reached around, and unhooked her bra, placing it on top of her shirt. Mesmerized, I tried to think of something to say. I watched as she arched her back and ran her hands through her hair, slowly shaking her head.

I realized this was for me. Another thought came to mind: this woman is no angel. She is a German Janet who, like Janet, lives for the moment and gets what she wants by doing whatever it takes. I thought there was something about me she desired. I now knew it wasn't me, but the antiviral for her animals. She bought into my ruse that I was under heavy pressure with a demanding schedule. She was willing to do whatever was necessary to corner me here until she had the medicine and her animals treated. I got mad at myself. What a naïve idiot I was!

These people are dog-eat-dog, no-hold-barred types of individuals, and she was one of the best. That's why Brian and Janet targeted her. It was a big game they took too seriously, as Brian had explained to me long ago. And now I was in the middle of it. I also knew that right now, I had the advantage. To her, I was another trophy. I gazed upon her perfect nude body and flawless, innocent face; I was going to turn the tables. There was no love, emotion, or genuine caring among these people, only the hunt and the kill.

Maria moved to the edge of the hot spring. Before she entered, she turned to look at me with raised eyebrows and her cute smile. She nodded her head for me to join her. I took a moment to take in the surroundings, still pondering my thoughts. She entered the water slowly and settled in, scooping water over her shoulders and neck.

I slipped off my desert boots and then my socks. I stood, undid my trousers, and shook them out. Taking my time, I took off my shirt. Nude, I moved to the side of the water and looked down at her as she unashamedly checked out my naked body. The water was hot but tolerable. Immersed, I dunked my head, relishing the cleansing water as it swept the dust and sweat of the journey from my face. I moved to the opposite side of the pool.

"It's nice having you here," she teased.

She pushed herself through the water. She gently clutched my knees, then pulled herself on top of me, putting her arms around my neck. I brought my hands up either side of her ribs, feeling her smooth skin as our lips met in a lingering kiss. I was an actor in a play, playing my part well. My hands found the softness of her bare bum and tenderly squeezed. I pulled her closer and felt her breasts against mine. I thought this wasn't a bad scene for an actor in a play.

We kissed and fondled each other in the naturally heated pool as time lost meaning. The heat began to take its toll, and we both knew that underwater wasn't a good place to finish.

Maria squeezed my cheeks and quickly kissed my lips. "We must get back. Clare will begin to worry. We'll miss dinner." She climbed out of the pool, looking at me by the water's edge. "You are wonderful," reaching down to help me up.

I immersed myself one more time. I reached for her hand and allowed her to pull me up, dripping in the cool air.

"We've got to hurry." she said.

I wondered how I was going to dry myself. Maria put her clothes back on, dripping wet, and I, having no other choice, did the same.

Maria put the food bits and empty wine bottles back in the bag. I struggled to get my pants on over my wet legs and bum. The socks were no easy task, not to mention struggling back into my desert boots. I stood and pulled my shirt over my head while Maria was already on her way back down the trail. I zipped up and buttoned my pants.

Down the steep path was no easier than coming up, sliding halfway down. Maria mounted and held my reins when I got there.

We turned the horses towards the ranch, and we started on a fast trot. When we reached the waterfall, Maria kicked her horse to a gallop. In the open field, we raced to the house. She beat me by a length as the sun sank below the horizon.

In the kitchen, Clare was checking pheasants in the oven. Looking up, "Drinks in twenty minutes."

Maria stopped to check out the baking birds. "They look splendid, Clare," she said.

The aroma filled the kitchen as Clare looked at me. "Fantastic," I said.

"I think they will do," Clare said, closing the oven door.

"We're going to clean up," said Maria.

Maria took my hand and led me to the great room, where she kissed my lips.

"See you in a bit," she said, entering her bedroom. She left me standing there.

I noticed that the table was set for eight.

CHAPTER 33

I knew I needed to turn this visit to culinary interests. I couldn't erase the picture of Maria lying on top of me, instigating our lovemaking. This adventure had gone beyond a prank; it became an emotional roller coaster I had never anticipated.

A group congregated around a table with drinks in the great room, helping themselves. The fire pit was aflame. The two Frenchmen, the Romanian couple and one of the Spanish girls, were engaged in lively conversation. When they noticed me, the conversation ceased, and the girls greeted me with hugs and kisses. The men held out their hands except François. Maria wasn't there.

As I mixed my drink, a Spanish girl asked, "How do you like Mariposa?"

"A special place," I answered.

"I love it here."

"Do you come here often?" I asked.

"As often as I can."

"Where do you live?"

"In Santiago. I work for the Spanish Embassy."

"That sounds demanding."

"Not really. I shuffle papers."

The door to the kitchen opened when Maria and Henny brought out plates of hors d'oeuvres and placed them on the table.

Maria approached me, "I see you got a drink."

"I did. Let me get you one."

"I'll take chardonnay. It's in the ice bucket."

The Romanian couple approached Maria and started a conversation. I joined them, handing Maria her drink. They were speaking German.

"Thank you." Smiling at me, they switched to English.

"This is Vasile and Ana. I don't think you have officially met."

"No, we haven't." holding out my hand to Vasile. "Where are you from?"

Shaking hands, "Romania," he answered.

Ana held out her hand, "Where are you from?"

"California."

"We haven't been to the United States," as she looked at Vasile. "I hear you are here to study llamas?"

"Yes, I am."

Maria excused herself and went back into the kitchen. I followed her with my eyes, then continued the conversation, explaining my mission.

Maria and Henny came through the kitchen door carrying two plates each of the main dishes, placing them at the settings of the dining table. Each setting had a place card for seating.

When the main dishes were set, Henny announced, "Please bring your drinks and find your seats."

My name was at the head of the table, and Maria was next to me. I waited to sit until the women were seated. Maria came up behind me, placing her hand on my shoulder.

"Please sit down."

Clare came from the kitchen and stood behind the seat at the other end of the table.

She explained, "Cherubs, tonight we have herb-roasted pheasant with wild rice and apricot stuffing. The side is cider-braised Brussels sprouts with bacon and apple. Please partake."

Then Clare took her seat, and Henny circled the table, filling glasses with white wine.

The plate included white and dark pheasant meat cuts, with stuffing on the side and a dab of homemade cranberry sauce to heighten the flavor.

Next to the pheasant, the braised Brussels sprouts were neatly laid out.

The presentation was high class. Clare knew her stuff. I cut a piece of pheasant, combined it with dressing, and dipped it into the cranberry sauce. The flavors were explosive. I tasted every ingredient, but none was overpowering a sweet combination. Next came the Brussels sprouts with the same results.

I looked at Clare as she watched me and raised my bourbon to her. She smiled and raised her glass as we toasted. The rest of the guests joined in congratulating Clare on a tantalizing meal.

Now was the time to get down to business, execute my plan, and change my focus from llamas to cooking.

"Do you eat like this every day?" I asked.

Maria laughed, "It depends on who is here. The kitchen is open to all to fend for themselves. Someone will prepare a meal once or twice weekly to show off a new recipe. You were lucky to get Clare."

"I take it that cooking is one of the major activities here at Mariposa?"

"It's a fun pastime evaluating each other's skill."

"Your place is world-renowned by the company you keep."

"We get guests from exotic places. Keeps the place humming."

"Do you have a specialty?"

"I do."

She quickly moved on, which was amusing. Knowing the game, she wasn't giving out too much information.

"I was curious when you mentioned you enjoyed working in the kitchen," Maria started.

"I started as a kid cooking my own breakfast."

"That's not surprising, coming from San Francisco. Do you have a specialty?"

"I enjoy doing seafood dishes."

"The fish market in San Francisco is unbelievable. I love going there. Which of your seafood dishes do you like the best?" she asked.

I had her hooked. There was no reason to hold back and act coy. I didn't have secrets; the Salmon Oyster Wrap was bait.

"My Salmon Oyster Wrap is the dish I'm most proud of."

"Salmon Oyster Wrap, very complementary."

"It can be. Took me a while to master it."

"I'd love to try it. What does it take?"

"Salmon and oysters."

"I figured that," she laughed. "What do you wrap it in?"

"I wrap the oyster in a very thin slice of salmon."

"Oh my God! Sounds incredible. Anything else?"

"I make a sauce to drizzle over the top."

"You have got to put this together while you're here."

"That might be tough, I only have another day or two, plus I don't have any oysters or salmon. The salmon must be fresh."

"I think we can work that out. I can have Juan pick up oysters on his way back from Santiago," she explained.

She looked over to François, "Y avait-il des poissons dans la rivière?"

"Oui il en avait, Les deux gars américains étaient là-bas."

"Tu veux dire Tom et Dave?"

"Oui ils me nerveux alors je suis parti."

I picked up what they said and heard Tom and Dave's names. I knew they were working their way up the river, which concerned me. I didn't want Maria to know I had encountered them and that this new twist could cause problems.

Maria turned and looked at me, "François says there is fish in the river. How much fishing have you done?"

"Quite a bit. In fact, I brought fishing gear with me because I heard the fishing here is surprisingly good and hoped to take advantage of it."

"We have a great steelhead run every year. These rivers are known for it. People come from all over the world to fish. François says there were two Americans fishing this morning. After we take the samples in the morning, we'll go down and try our luck. What do you say?"

"We can try it. I can substitute the steelhead for the salmon."

"I'm looking forward to those salmon or steelhead oyster wraps."

I was about to explode as I realized how easily they took the bait. I lifted my wine glass, looked at Maria, and toasted, "Steelhead Oyster Wraps tomorrow."

Everyone laughed and joined in on this toast.

CHAPTER 34

I was concerned about Tom and Dave being in the area. I picked up from Maria and François that Tom and Dave made Francois nervous. Why, I didn't know. Was there more to Tom and Dave being in the area than fishing? I remembered what Tom had said when I mentioned that I was coming to Maria's and that they would look after me. What did that mean?

The last and most crucial issue was enticing Maria to share her chili relleno recipe. I had to play my cards with this Salmon Oyster Wrap and somehow get her to reciprocate.

The dinner party was breaking up. Guests, including François and his partner, began to go to their rooms. I was tired and wanted to call it a night.

I thanked Clare for a wonderful meal. She kissed my cheek and said, "I'm so glad you're here. I'm looking forward to that steelhead wrap."

"It depends if we catch any fish tomorrow," I laughed.

"I'm sure you will," she concluded.

Maria reached out to say goodnight, and I asked, "What are the plans for tomorrow?"

"We'll get up early and get the blood samples and send them off, and then I'll take you down to the river. François was going to come, but he decided not to."

It was a relief to hear he wasn't coming, but trying to be friendly, I faked a disappointed look, "Why not?"

"Because of the two Americans fishing down there."

"I take it you've met them?"

"I met them at Ricardo's. They're nice enough, but François thinks they're CIA agents."

"Why would that bother François?"

"Because François is a devout communist."

"How do you feel about that?"

"I don't know if you are aware of what's happening in Chile politically."

"Not really," I lied.

"At the moment, there is a clash between right-wing and left-wing political parties that is starting to turn violent."

"What's that got to do with François?"

"He is a radical and went to Santiago University to organize demonstrations, which put him in the military spotlight. They don't like outsiders starting trouble."

"What's he doing here?"

"He asked if he could come and hang out for a while until the situation calmed down."

"Doesn't that put you in an awkward position?"

"I shouldn't be telling you this, but since you asked, I'm not worried. My father's legacy goes far back, and he has influential connections that look after me. François is a very dear friend. I couldn't say no when he asked me. Now you know the whole story."

With no further comment, I looked at her. "Thank you for everything," thinking it was the end of a lovely evening.

She squeezed my hand and looked like she hadn't finished yet.

This added dimension Maria told me about François weighed on my mind. But for the alcohol I drank at dinner, I might be in a panic.

It dawned on me that Tom and Dave might be CIA agents scoping out François. Could there be trouble by association?

About to fall asleep, my door slowly opened. "Now what?" I thought. I opened my eyes to see Maria standing in the dim light. She untied her robe and let it drop to the floor, standing nude. She pulled the door shut and came to the side of the bed, lifted the covers, slid in, and put her arms around me.

"Hi, Baby."

Her lips compassed mine, darting her tongue into my mouth. Not resisting, we finished what started at the hot springs, falling asleep in each other's arms.

CHAPTER 35

A knock on the door. I wrestled to wake up in the darkness. Maria was gone. The knock came again, with Henny's voice, "Good morning, Tony," with another knock.

I struggled into my pants. "Hang on a minute." Finding the light, shirtless, I opened the door.

"It's time to go fishing. Breakfast is in the kitchen."

Shaking the cobwebs from my brain, I said, "Give me a minute. I'll be right there." It was 5 a.m.

Henny walked away.

Savoring the thoughts of the night, I found my fishing gear. Dressed and refreshed as I could be, I carried my gear to the empty kitchen, where the table was set with a scone, butter, and jam on one plate. On another, cut salami and cheese next to a bowl of sliced pears, steaming coffee to the side.

When the kitchen door opened, I wondered where everyone was. It was Maria. Again, my mouth was full of scones. She placed her arms on my shoulders, bent down, and kissed my neck.

Not lingering, she walked out the back door, "I'll be right back."

Unable to say anything with my mouth full, I finished breakfast as she returned, "We're set. Are you ready?"

"Yep," I answered.

I picked up the pack and gear. Maria held open the door for me and puckered her lips to receive a kiss.

Dawn was breaking, the horses were waiting, and we mounted. Juan waited for us at the barn. It didn't take long to take the samples of three animals. I wrapped them in wax paper, placed them in a box, and handed them to Juan in the Range Rover. We watched him leave for Santiago.

Maria led the way across the field toward the river. There was no mention of the encounter the night before. It was getting lighter as we reached the end of the field and the trail down to the river.

The sound of rushing water came from a series of rapids in the river below. The trail was steep. The horses went slow. At the river's edge, smooth water separated a set of rapids. I dismounted and removed the fishing gear and attached the rod sections. I ran a line through the guides. I found one I liked from the tin of flies and tied it off. I was ready to fish.

Maria watched me, then commented, "A lot of people fish this spot. Some big ones came out of here."

"We need a ten-pounder to get the filets for the oyster wrap."

I moved up the river below a rapid and let out more line with each cast. The fly drifts downstream, yielding nothing. I cast it repeatedly, and without luck, I tried the water downriver. My first cast the fly hooked onto the back of my vest. Embarrassed, I looked at Maria. She tried not to chuckle.

"It happens," I said.

"It does," she laughed.

I worked down below the rapid. I hoped I'd have a fish by now. Frustration welled up as I kept casting… nothing.

Two people were fishing downriver and approaching me. Maria noticed them. "That looks like the Americans, Tom and Dave," she announced.

Tom and Dave, I thought, what a horrible time to run into those guys. They'd recognize me and want to talk. How would I explain to Maria how I met them? I thought about changing directions, but it seemed too obvious. Plus, I fished those areas, and there was nothing. I had to produce something quickly, and they were coming up fast.

I'd have to tell Maria the truth. There was nothing wrong with taking a little time out fishing.

On the next cast, "Tom and Dave, I met them in Coya when passing through."

"You met them?"

"I went fishing with them one morning."

"How well do you know them?" an inquisitive look on her face.

While she asked, a big fish broke the water. Landing would not be easy, and I had to work the line to keep it from being lost.

Maria ran to my side, squealing, "That's a big one! Don't lose it!"

I didn't answer, working on the fish. Tom and Dave noticed me fighting a big one. Hoping to help, they rolled in their lines and ran up to me.

"Looks like you got a giant," shouted Tom.

I looked at them briefly, acknowledging their presence, and worked the fish.

Maria shied away. I could tell she had an uneasy feeling about Tom and Dave. She probably wondered what my connection was with these two cowboys from Texas.

The fish came closer to shore. Dave brought his fish net to help. I stood knee-deep in the water as the fish surged. I let it run, to keep from snapping the line while wearing the fish out. The fish got tired, so I put more pressure on it. Finally, I reeled him in. Dave reached out with his net, lost his footing on the slick river bottom, and fell into me, knocking items from my pocket. He regained his footing and netted the beautiful twenty-pound steelhead trout.

I took the fish by the lower lip and lifted it to admire. I could hardly hold it up. It was so heavy. Maria was proud of me for landing such a fish.

Tom exclaimed, "Nice job! We've been fishing all morning and only got small ones."

"It's the biggest fish I've ever caught," I giggled.

Maria smiled, standing back, being illusive. Something changed.

"What are you going to do, keep it?" asked Tom.

"We have a special dinner planned up at the ranch."

"That will make quite a meal. Enjoy."

I wanted to quickly break away from Tom and Dave, "Thanks for your help, fellas. Don't mean to run, but we've got to get this fish back as soon as possible. Must keep it fresh."

"We understand. We have more fishing to do."

I started when Tom said, "Hey Tony, you dropped your tin of flies."

I checked my vest. The tin was missing. Tom didn't move but held up the tin, wanting me to come to him. Maria kept going. Laying the fish on the rocks, I returned to get the tin.

When I got to him, Tom asked, "Is there a Frenchman named François staying up there with you?"

Without thinking, I answered, "Yes." As soon as I did, I knew I made a mistake. "Why do you ask?"

We studied each other's faces. Tom said, "Just wondered."

Our gazes lingered for a moment, then I took the tin and put it in my pocket. "I've got to go. Thanks again."

"I hope to run into you again sometime. Have fun with that fish."

Rushing to pick up the gear and the fish, I could hardly carry it.

Maria turned to see me struggle and came back.

"Here, let me help." she offered.

She took the fishing pole, and we climbed up to the horses, me clutching the fish to my chest.

Maria had a worried look on her face, staring back at Tom and Dave.

There was more to this encounter than chance. When Tom said he'd be looking out for me, I remembered Coya. Tom made a point when he asked if François was at the ranch. Maria's response to Tom and Dave perplexed me. I was nervous about what would happen next. I had to keep going, but this new development wouldn't be easy.

It was a quiet ride to the ranch with the fish strapped behind the saddle. Maria was distracted. I didn't know what to do. I followed in her wake until we reached the veranda.

Maria stood quietly as I dismounted and unstrapped the fish.

Clare burst through the back door, "Oh my God!!! What a beautiful catch, did you catch that, Tony?"

Maria broke her silence, "He did. Isn't it grand?"

"Wonderful! Come bring it in!" holding the door open. "Lay it on the table. Oh my, how spectacular. This is cause for a toast," continued Clare, placing three wine glasses on the table and opening a bottle of red.

"You should have seen Tony land that fish. He was fantastic!"

"I had help," I admitted as Clare poured the wine and passed the glasses to each of us.

"A toast, then, to the mighty fisherman and good life… except for the poor fish, of course," added Clare.

Maria laughed as we clinked our glasses together and drank.

I downed the whole glass.

Clare refilled my glass. "You must be thirsty, ol' chap."

The wine calmed my nerves from the morning drama. I downed my second glass; Maria seemed relaxed, like her old self.

CHAPTER 36

Clare asked, "What do we do now? Shall we wait for the others?"

"I don't want to get started until the oysters get here."

Maria looked at the clock on the wall, "Juan should be back in a couple of hours."

The time had come to pull the trigger. I needed to be on top of the game. "A couple of hours, do you mind if I go to my room and take a nap? I feel like I've barely slept in days."

"Not at all. We want you fresh to perform your magic."

"If you'll excuse me," I turned to leave.

"Don't forget your wine. Take it with you," said Clare.

I carried my wine glass through the kitchen door. Maria followed me out, "Tony, please wait a minute."

She approached me and took my hand. "To let you know, I really enjoyed last night. You were great, and this morning's fishing I also enjoyed. I can hardly wait for this meal you're going to make. I wanted you to know that."

"I'm looking forward to it, too. Should be fun."

She kissed me. "Have a rest. See you in a bit."

I watched her return to the kitchen and took a drink. I felt like a man on the verge of combat. I went to my room and slept for two hours.

Awake, I looked at my watch, it was four-thirty. The hot shower felt good as I organized my thoughts, going over the steps needed for this meal.

I noticed asparagus in the garden as we rode by. Asparagus would go well with roasted walnuts and goat cheese melted over the top.

Quickly, I toweled off and put on fresh clothes. I went outside, and the Land Rover parked in front of the ranch house. "Good," I thought, "Juan is back with the oysters."

Clare and Henny admired the fish on the table. "There you are. Are you ready to proceed?" asked Clare.

"I am."

"What do I need to get for you?" Clare asked.

A bucket of oysters lay on the floor in front of the table. I examined one, "These are nice, just the right size."

"I need a really sharp knife," I said to Clare.

Clare reached into the cutlery block and chose one.

"Will this do?"

"Perfect."

Clare took out the steel and began sharpening it.

"I noticed asparagus in the garden. That will go with the meal."

Henny piped in, "I'll get them. How much do you need?"

"I'm not sure. What's the number of people we are feeding?"

"Around eight, I believe. Juan bought three dozen oysters. Figure four oysters apiece," said Clare.

"Pick a whole basket full, and we'll make it work. How about walnuts? Do we have walnuts?"

Clare looked toward the larder, "Plenty of walnuts."

"Goat cheese?"

"We have llama cheese."

"Let's get started."

Henny left to get the asparagus. I took the knife from Clare.

"Is there anything I can do to help?" she asked.

"You can chop up the walnuts and grate the cheese."

"Will do."

Clare came to the table with the walnuts and cheese as I cut the first piece of fish. She stopped to watch as I finished the filet.

"You are a master with that knife," Clare declared.

"Done this a few times, Clare."

"It shows," as she started to chop up the walnuts.

"This is the hard part." I cut the filet into thin slabs.

"You know, Clare, it's tough to do this without a glass of wine."

Maria suddenly walked in, showing her disappointment, "You started without me! I'll get the wine."

Clare chopped the walnuts, and Maria poured the wine while I sliced the filet into the super thin cuts. Holding the slice to the light, it was perfectly translucent. It was big enough to cut in half and wrap two oysters. Clare and Maria watched silently as I laid each slice in a fan. I took a drink and looked at the clock. It was a quarter to six.

I asked Maria, "What time do you want to eat?"

"Whenever you get finished."

"Let's go for sevenish."

Clare nodded her approval and kept chopping walnuts. Henny came in with a whole basket of asparagus.

"Clare, can you manage the asparagus?"

"What do you want me to do?"

"We need two baking pans. Put walnuts in one and roast them until crunchy. Place them in a bowl, and oil the pan with olive oil. Arrange the asparagus in rows to bake until soft. Spread the walnuts on top, grate cheese over them, and back in the oven until the cheese melts. Think you can manage that?"

"You silly boy. Why do you need the other pan?"

"I'll need that for the oyster wraps."

"Got it. Continue."

Maria sipped her wine, pulled up a chair, and sat, engrossed in the process.

The bucket of oysters was emptied on the table, and I took a bowl off the shelf.

Clare slid the chopped walnuts into the oven to bake, so I asked for an oyster knife.

Maria went to a drawer and rifled around until she found one.

"For the sauce over the wraps, I need dark mustard, grated ginger, and dill weed."

Maria could no longer sit idle, "I can do the sauce if you tell me what to do."

"Sure, get a bowl and put in...hmm." Thinking about what was needed, "Put in four or five tablespoons of olive oil, add the mustard. Mix it up until they come together. Grate the ginger over the top."

"How much?"

"We'll figure that out as you do it."

"Same with the dill weed?" she asked.

"Right."

I pried the hinge of the first oyster. It popped open, and the shells were scraped into the bowl. Then, I put the bucket on the floor.

Henny was eager to help, "Can I do something?"

Maria stirred the sauce. "You can set the table for eight. The Spanish couple, François and Pierre, and I are four."

Henny left to set the table.

Clare opened the oven and spooned baked walnuts, "How's this?"

I assessed the walnuts, "Almost; a bit longer." I answered.

Clare closed the oven door. Maria showed me the sauce. "That looks good. Add the ginger now."

Clare topped off the wine glasses.

After shucking the oysters, I said, "Clare, we don't want to cook these wraps too long, just enough to stiffen them."

She removed the roasted walnuts, put them in a bowl, and oiled the pan, adding the asparagus. Maria added dill weed to her mix, stirred it in, and offered it to me to evaluate.

"A bit more ginger."

With the asparagus in the oven, it was time to wrap the oysters. After oiling the baking pan, I tried the sauce again. "Perfect."

Oyster wraps filled the pan. "We're ready to cook. Let's check the asparagus."

Clare placed the asparagus on the table. Cooked perfectly, roasted walnuts are spread evenly over them.

"Clare, grate a good amount of cheese over the top, and put it back in the oven."

"Do we put on the sauce now?" asked Maria,

I placed the wraps in the oven. "No, we'll let them cook and brush the butter on the tops; we want them moist. We'll cook them for ten minutes and then check them."

Across from Maria, I sat down with my wine.

Clare excused herself, "I'll go help Henny get the table ready."

"How did you come up with this recipe?" asked Maria.

"You better wait to ask that question after you taste it," I laughed.

"I'm sure it's flavorful. The combination is art in itself."

I thought back to when Brian produced it on the houseboat. I felt guilty, claiming it for myself, but this was the game, the ruse.

I wanted to use this moment to get the chili relleno recipe. Carelessly, I mumbled, "I'm sure you have a specialty you're hiding. It would be nice to compare."

Maria changed the subject, "We'd better check on those wraps. Is it time to put the asparagus back in?"

I opened the oven as Maria came around to see the results. I slid the tray halfway out, "They look ready for the sauce. Have you a basting brush?"

She removed a one-inch brush from the drawer, "How much do you apply?"

"Not too much. We don't want to overpower the wrap."

I brushed sauce on each wrap, pushed the tray into the oven, and slid in the asparagus to melt the cheese. It was ten to seven. "We should be ready to eat in fifteen minutes," I said.

"I hear people rumbling around in the dining room. I think we should prepare the plates here and take them out," Maria suggested.

"I was thinking the same thing."

I wrestled with what to do next. This was my trump card, and there was no indication that she would reciprocate. The political intrigue had me nervous. I was over my head, and I had no graceful exit plan. I began to wonder why I let Janet talk me into this. It seemed so simple at first.

Maria came in with the plates. Clare was behind her. "Okay, Tony," Clare blurted, "Time to present your masterpiece."

The wraps and asparagus looked perfect.

Clare proclaimed, "It looks absolutely yummy."

Maria agreed, "It does look good. Can't wait."

Gently lifting the wraps off the pan and placing four wraps on each plate, we added six asparagus stalks with the roasted walnuts and melted llama cheese.

We placed the plates on the table, and the seated guests admired my creation.

Henny topped off the wine glasses.

Clare, taking control, stood behind her chair and said, "It's in good order to toast the chef, I'd say!"

She lifted her glass; the others did the same.

Embarrassed, I looked at Clare and said, "It might be better to wait until you taste it first."

"Oh, balderdash!" she admonished, drinking her wine.

"Bon appetit, please partake," I announced.

They tasted the wrap with mixed reactions, and I was never good at reading people. I looked at Maria; this was the actual test. Did I do enough to impress her? This was the reason I was here.

She placed a piece in her mouth, discerning the flavor.

She took another bite, then a third. She swallowed and then looked at me, "I was worried the sauce would overpower the fish and oyster, but the combination works out well."

"You think so?"

"I do."

Looking at the Frenchman, Maria asks, "What do you think, François?"

"The asparagus is very good," looking at me with a smirk.

I gave him the middle finger, "Very funny."

The table broke out in laughter. I relaxed and enjoyed the rest of the meal. It was a hit with Maria, and that's what mattered. Confused, I wondered where to go from here.

After finishing their meals, people began to mingle. They expressed their appreciation for such a fine work of art. Even François shook my hand and expressed his gratitude. Maria looked on with pride.

Later in the evening, people went to their rooms. Clare and Henny were cleaning up in the kitchen.

"Anything I can do?" I asked.

"Of course not. Job well done. Just splendid."

"Thanks."

I turned to leave, but Maria came and put her arm around mine, asking, " Is everything okay in here?"

"We're almost finished. You go on," said Clare.

We sat on the couch next to the fire pit. Maria interlaced her fingers in mine, "Do you mind if I ask how long you think it will take to get the results from the samples?"

"I'm not sure. A couple of days, I suppose."

"Is it possible for you to stay until they come in?"

"Why do you ask?"

"For two reasons. One, I like your company, and two, I'd like to follow through in hopes that my animals heal."

CHAPTER 37

The end of this caper hit me like a ton of bricks. At a loss to figure out how to get this recipe out of her, my only alternative was to play hardball, no holds barred, and bribe her with the recipe for the serum. First, I had to know I could follow through with my end of the deal. I had to talk to Janet to work this deal out. I needed more time.

"You know, if the samples come back positive for the A24, I don't have the serum. That would have to come from the States, " I said.

"I know, but I'd like you to be here to see the results. I'm hoping that Dr. Wasson can use my animals for a test case."

"That's a clever idea, but I'd have to ask him. I'll support you, but to get the serum is out of my hands."

"I know that, and I can't thank you enough for what you've already done." She paused. "I loved your oyster wraps. Come on. It's late. I'll walk you to your room."

At my door, she turned and put her arms around me, planting her lips on mine for a lingering kiss. Our lips parted, and I asked, "Do I get another mystery visit tonight?"

She winked, "We'll see," then she turned and walked away.

Lying in bed, my thoughts returned to the bribe. It would change the whole dynamic. Could I be that cold-hearted? I had feelings for Maria, but I knew that would change once she discovered who I was.

The other option was to walk away, admit defeat, and escape this situation. It was a game, anyway. I helped with the samples; if the A24 worked, it did well. Brian and Janet would be disappointed, but they'd get over it. I'd call Janet and tell her the options tomorrow, but then I fell asleep.

CHAPTER 38

A horrible racket woke me up from the front of the ranch. I jumped up, turned on the light, and put on my pants. My door burst open, and two uniformed men entered my room holding automatic weapons. Forcibly, they grabbed me under the armpits and muscled me to the front yard, where six white Ford Falcons lined up with more men scurrying around.

Other men searched the house for something. Maria was screaming from inside. Terrified, three men came out the front door, pushing François out the portico onto the lawn. Others gathered around François as one opened the rear door of a white Falcon, forcing him into the back seat, shouting and yelling.

A uniformed man yelled a command, and the men got in the cars and sped off.

Maria screamed as she ran out and chased the cars on foot. She realized her chase was futile, so she stopped, put her hands to her face, bent over, and cried out, "NO, NO!!!" hysterically weeping.

Clare and Henny stood on the porch and looked terrified. Clare ran down to Maria and put her arms around her in comfort. Dumbfounded, I stood barefoot and shirtless. I didn't know what to do or think.

Clare turned Maria around and led her back into the house. She cried with her hands covering her face.

I stood alone in the chilly night air. I had to do something. It became clear that Tom and Dave worked with the Chilean government. They were CIA agents who chased after François for anti-government activities.

I would be in deep trouble if Maria assumed I was involved in this drama. I wanted to run, but with nowhere to go, I had to face the music and play it out the best I could. I put on my shoes and went to the house.

Maria sat on the leather couch crying. Clare held her in her arms. Henny and others stood around with frightful looks on their faces.

My worst fears became a reality as Maria, with hate in her eyes, looked up at me and screamed, "YOU'RE A PART OF THIS, YOU FUCKING SPY!!!"

Clare looked at me, "YOU BASTARD!"

I felt helpless; Henny, with a look of mercy and concern on her face, seemed to understand and come to my aid.

"I don't think Tony is a spy. He could have had François arrested when he brought Tony to the ranch."

Maria, not convinced, looked up at me.

"What were you and Tom talking about down at the river? You'd better explain yourself!"

The gig was up. The only way out was to tell the truth and get out the best I could.

I waited before answering as they glared at me. The atmosphere was thick.

"Well!" Maria demanded an answer.

I tried to figure out where to start, "I am a spy."

Once again, Clare yelled, "YOU BASTARD!"

"But not for the CIA."

The room went quiet.

"If you're not with the CIA, who are you a spy for?"

There was another painful silence before I answered, "I had nothing to do with those guys! I ran into them the other day in Coya. I thought they were two cowboys from Texas down here fishing. I'm spying for Brian and Janet."

Maria looked confused, "You mean Brian Williams and Janet Legrand!!!"

I nodded, "Yes."

"What in the world did they send you to spy on me for?"

"Your Chili Relleno recipe."

Maria put her hands on her face, put her head back on the couch, and laughed hysterically. Clare looked on in bewilderment.

Maria got control of herself, "You mean Brian and Janet went to all this expense and trouble for a recipe? OH MY GOD!"

"Yes, they did."

"And they talked you into doing it?"

"Yes."

"You came all this way for a prank?"

"I did."

"You don't have anything better to do?"

"Actually, I wasn't doing anything, and it seemed like a good idea at the time."

"So, the whole A24 story is fake?"

"No! That was part of Janet's plan. She worked it out with Dr. Wasson."

"Janet came up with this, and the A24 is real?"

"She did, and it's real!"

"This is crazy," and began to laugh again. "How did you plan to get the recipe?"

"I hoped you'd fall in love with me and give it to me if I asked. But I realized that wasn't going to work, so I was going to come clean and trade you the A24 for the recipe."

"You were going to bribe me?"

"Yes, I was."

Clare burst out again, "YOU BASTARD!"

Maria laughed again as I stood there and felt foolish.

"What did Tom say to you down on the river?"

"He asked me if François was up at the ranch."

"And you told him?"

"I did."

"That's the problem. That's where this came from. Tom and Dave are spies."

"I knew I blew it when I told him."

After a brief silence, Maria looked at me, "Just for the record, I've grown very fond of you."

"That's been my dilemma. I've become very fond of you, Maria."

Our eyes lingered on each other, but Maria broke off the contact. "We must do something to get François back. They will mistreat him."

I thought for a second, "I think I can help."

"How's that?"

"I need to make a phone call to the States."

We stood from the couch, and she took my hand, "Come. You can call from my office."

Maria motioned toward her desk inside the office, "Sit down." She picked up the phone. "What's the number?"

She dialed as I quoted the number. The phone began to ring, and she handed it to me, saying, "I'll leave you alone." She turned and left the room.

Janet picked up the phone. "Hello."

"Janet, Tony."

"Tony! How's it going?"

"Not good."

"What do you mean?"

"The police raided Maria's place and arrested François. We've got to get him back."

"You mean François from Marseilles?"

"Yes, that's him."

"Oh shit. He's such an idiot. Better to leave him with the police."

"We can't. It all depends on getting him out."

"What are you talking about?"

"I don't have time to explain, but believe me, if we get him out, I'm sure I can get the recipe."

"What do you want me to do?"

"Call your brother and have him put diplomatic pressure on the Chilean government to release him. Tell him to call his French communist connections. I'm sure they'll want him back."

"That's a big assignment. I'll get on it right now. When this is over, I want to hear about it."

"Don't worry, I'll tell you everything. Now get hot."

I hung up with Janet and returned to the living room, feeling uncomfortable as they stared at me.

"Now, we must wait. I suggest we go to bed. Nothing more we can do right now," I advised.

"I won't be able to sleep," cried Maria, "But you go on."

I excused myself, went to the sanctity of my room, and locked the door, fearful the police might return. My emotions ran high, and I was relieved it was over and I didn't have to lie anymore. What a mess! I couldn't have felt more stupid or deceitful.

Two hours passed when I received a knock on my door: "Tony, it's me. May I come in? I have news."

I unlocked the door. Maria rushed past me and sat on the bed, "I got a call from François. They released him. The police are sending a car to pick up his things. They are deporting him back to France."

"You've got to be kidding!"

"I don't know what you did, but it worked."

"I can't believe it happened so fast!"

She stood up, hugged me, and kissed my lips. "I have something for you in the kitchen. Come when you're ready."

Behind the table, Maria faced the stove and stirred what looked like tomato sauce. On the table were four green chilies, a block of llama cheese, four eggs, two bowls, and a whisk. The block of cheese looked like the llama cheese Alec had used for his quesadillas.

"Is this llama cheese?" I asked

She turned, "It's the secret you came down here to find."

I rounded the table to join her. She pinched off a piece of cheese and placed it between my lips as she stirred the sauce. The cheese melted in my mouth, and it had a unique taste.

"I'll show you how to do this," she said.

"Chili Relleno?"

"You earned it."

A skillet on the stove held a quarter cup of heated olive oil. She added two tablespoons of sifted flour and a quarter cup of ground red chilies and stirred, not allowing the mixture to burn.

While working, she said, "When the flour turns light brown, add the tomato sauce and 1.5 cups of water. Add a quarter teaspoon of ground cumin, crushed garlic, and onion salt. Stir it to a light boil."

"What are you making here?" I asked.

"This is the enchilada sauce to go over the rellenos."

"You came up with this recipe?"

"It's been around for a while, but I change it now and again for something different. After a light boil, set it aside on the range top to keep it warm. Delicately separate six egg whites from the yolks into two bowls. Place the chilies on a burner to scald off the skins. Slice one side down the middle, leaving them whole, and scrape out the seeds with a small spoon. She cut healthy slices of the llama cheese, placed them inside the chilies, and set them aside. She poured vegetable oil an inch deep into a small skillet and put it on a warm spot on the stove to heat up. They whisked the egg whites into a thick meringue.

"This is another secret no one can figure out, whisked egg whites?"

"Once the whites are fluffy and stiff, whisk the yolks thoroughly, gently folding them into the meringue.

"Sift flour into the meringue to thicken it, but don't overdo it. Be gentle, or the mix will go flat."

"This is part of the mystery?"

"That and my sauce nobody can match."

"No doubt," I responded, taking it all in.

She turned to the stove and said, "Place the oiled skillet over the flame, the oil hot. Scoop a bit of meringue with your finger and flick it into the oil to evaluate the heat. When the meringue begins to sizzle, dip the cheese-stuffed chili into the meringue until fully covered, and tenderly lower it into the hot oil to cook. Make sure the top and bottom brown evenly. Do not overcook; just enough to melt the cheese."

I went over the process, "A fine piece of work."

She pointed with her chin to the stack of plates, "Could you get two plates and hold them for me?"

"Pick up the evenly browned rellenos with a screen spatula and hold over the skillet allowing the excess oil to drain, and place each on the plate. Give the sauce a quick stir and pour it over the rellenos until it dribbles down the sides. Then top them with more grated llama cheese."

She placed the plates on the table, ready to eat.

She handed me a cup of coffee, "Have a seat."

She allowed me to take the first bite, and I cut a healthy piece of relleno. The taste was nothing I imagined, and my effort and agony became worth it. Eating this masterpiece, I had a strange thought: I don't want to share this recipe; I want to keep it for myself. I felt sorry for Maria. She had lost. I violated her for a game. I didn't have the cold heart needed for this kind of life.

Henny burst into the kitchen and said, "Tony, you have a phone call from the University, Doctor Herrera."

Looking at Maria. "Let's hope this is good news."

Maria said, "Let's find out," and led me to the office. Henny followed behind. She handed me the receiver, anxious to hear the news.

"Hello, yes, this is Tony Taylor... Yes, Doctor Herrera, it's nice to hear from you.... I see, that's wonderful news. You say it will arrive next week. That's great! I'm sure Maria will be excited... Yes, I'll tell her."

Maria squealed excitedly, taking Henny in a bear hug, and they danced around the room.

CHAPTER 39

Two months later, the phone rang in my hotel room in Valencia, Spain. I picked it up as I looked over the water at the large luxury yacht anchored in the harbor.

"Hello, Darling, I landed in Madrid."

"How was your flight?"

"No problems, long as usual. I catch the train in an hour. Should be there in time for dinner. Can you see the yacht?"

"I saw the yacht, and Henny got on with the kitchen staff in the galley."

"How did that happen?"

"Janet, as usual. You know she works miracles."

"Are we on the dinner list?"

"Another work of Janet's."

"That's great, Sweetie. With Henny in the galley, we should be able to crack this caper."

"I'm sure of it. See you when you get here."

"I love you, Baby."

How easily and flatly those words slid from Maria's lips. I nodded silently over the phone as if she could hear it.

There came a knock on my door. François stood in the hall.

Maria invited him to join this adventure and reserved a room for him. Although I didn't like the idea, I wasn't the one who made the rules.

"Did Maria call you?" asked François.

Irked by his presence, "She said she was on her way."

"She called me too. Wanted to see if you got the call."

Why does this Frenchman have to be involved? Maria knew I didn't like him, but she insisted on it. It was a burr under my saddle that made me feel insecure with our relationship. I felt like a trophy rather than the man in her life.

Janet arranged this caper, and I was a puppet on a string between the two women. Hobnobbing with the rich and famous was very important to them, but I was tired of it. It was the sex that held me captive. Months ago, that wasn't objectionable, but my friendship with Whiskey reshaped my thinking as time went on.

François looked at me and said, "I'm going to the pub for a drink. Would you like to join me?"

I was going to the pub, but since François asked, I changed my mind, "Not right now, maybe later," and shut the door.

I looked out the window at the anchored yacht, perplexed. The phone rang again. I picked up the receiver, "Yes?"

The concierge at the front desk said, "Mr. Taylor, Janet has called you from the United States. Do you wish to take the call?"

"Of course, put her on."

I heard Janet's voice, "Tony, I have bad news."

"Bad news, what do you mean, bad news?"

"It's Whiskey. He hasn't been feeling well, and it looks like the situation has gotten worse."

Whiskey wasn't in the best health, and he looked a little more diminished each time I visited. I begged him to go to the doctor, but he refused and insisted it was nothing. He'd get over it.

"It's his heart. Brian is with him and said it looks like he is at death's door."

"My God!" I gasped, taken aback by this news.

"Another thing," Janet continued, "He keeps asking for you."

I had to do something! The little guy had nobody. The only people he knew were at the marina, and now, with Maud gone, who would be there for him? He had asked for me as I sat in a hotel in Spain and played a foolish game.

"What should I do?" I thought aloud, "Should I call him?"

"That might help. Brian thinks he could go at any time."

I had to get there immediately, and nothing else mattered. It was complicated, and I needed Janet's help.

"I'm going to get back for him. You're going to have to help me,"

"Sounds like I don't have a choice."

"That's right. I know there is a midnight flight to New York, and I'm going to be on it and connect to San Francisco from there. You have to arrange it for me."

"What if I can't?" she responded.

"You pull off miracles when it's something you want to happen. Now, you're going to have to do this for me and Whiskey. You have to make it happen."

I didn't wait for her response: "I'm going to pack up and get to the train station. It'll be the same train Maria comes in on, and I'll explain to her that I need to be on that plane. When I get to San Francisco, I want you to pick me up at the airport so I can go directly to Whiskey's place. We might not have too much time."

Janet answered as if it were a done deal, "Should I tell Whiskey you are coming?"

"Yes, it might keep him going. I'll see you when I get there."

I hung up the phone, packed up my bag, and took the room keys to the front desk to check out.

Francois sat at the bar as I passed by.

I shouted, "Hey, François."

Confused, François turned, my pack flung over my shoulder.

"I'm taking off."

"What do you mean you're taking off?"

"I'm taking off," I repeated.

"How can you take off? You have dinner tonight with Maria on the yacht."

I didn't explain myself, "An emergency came up at home. I've got to go."

"That's fucking crazy. Can't you wait until tomorrow?"

"It might be too late. I'll tell you what is fucking crazy. This whole fucking scene is crazy. You go to dinner with Maria. She'll be more than happy to have you."

I left François at the bar, his expression stunned, and walked through the hotel doors to a waiting taxi.

I bought a train ticket for Madrid and followed the signs to the correct platform. Maria would get off the train, and I would get on. I no longer cared what Maria thought or how she'd respond. I was doing the right thing and felt good for the first time in a long time.

The train noisily rolled up to the platform. The doors opened, and Maria, carrying her luggage, was the first person off. She immediately noticed me as I stood with my pack and ticket. Surprised, she ran up, dropped her luggage, hugged me, and kissed my lips. She was confused when I didn't respond.

"What the hell is going on?" were the first words out of her mouth.

"I must go. There's an emergency I need to attend to."

"An emergency?" she stammered, "What kind of an emergency?"

"A friend of mine is dying, and I have to go."

It took a moment for it to register. She raised her voice, "I can't believe it! This has been set up. You can't imagine how disappointed I am. I was so excited about going to dinner on the yacht with you, and now suddenly, you must leave?"

"I can't explain it to you, Maria. Trust me. I must go; François will be with you on the yacht."

The conductor yelled, "Todos a bordo."

"I've got to go," I dodged around her to get on the train.

I stepped onto the train, and Maria yelled, "If you get on that train, I never want to see you again!"

I looked back blankly and yelled, "You know Maria, it's only a game."

I took my seat. Maria stared after me as the train left and headed for Madrid.

At the Pan Am ticket counter, I presented my passport to the ticket agent, who then checked the passenger list.

"Mr. Taylor. Window or aisle seat?"

"Window, please."

Janet pulled it off despite spoiling her carefully constructed plans.

On the flight over the Atlantic, wracked with mixed feelings, I realized Maria and I were never a couple. I was good for her until the next guy came along. I felt determined that Janet and I must go our separate ways. I was tired of playing the game. It was time to stand on my own two feet. My main concern was Whiskey, and I hoped I'd return in time.

I arrived in San Francisco on time, in the late morning. Janet was waiting for me.

She didn't hug or kiss me, "We've got to hurry. He's not doing well. It looks like he could go at any moment."

Relieved Whiskey was still alive, we rushed to Janet's car.

We ran to Whiskey's open door at the marina and rushed in. Brian sat next to Whiskey and held his hand. Harold stood next to the door. At the bedside, I knelt beside him. Whiskey looked ashen, his breathing labored, his eyes barely opened. The little dog rested in the crook of his arm, a worried look on his furry little face.

Brian squeezed the weak, ashen hand, "Whiskey, Tony is here."

Whiskey opened his eyes and looked up. "Tony," he uttered in a half-whispered voice as a weak smile crossed his face. He released Brian's grip to reach for mine.

I took Whiskey's hand, held it with one, and rubbed it with the other. I glanced at Brian. He shook his head, confirming that the end was near.

Whiskey closed his eyes and laid his head back, holding my hand. After an eternity, he opened his eyes and looked at me. With all the strength he could muster, "I love you, Tony. I'm so glad you came. This is about it for old Whiskey." A faint smile returned on his face.

"I love you, too, Whiskey. You're a good friend."

"I need you to do me a couple of favors."

"Of course, I can. What are they?"

"I'm worried about Billy; I want to make sure he is cared for. Can you promise you'll find a good person who loves him the way I do?"

"We will. You don't have to worry. What else?"

"I'll be next to Maud, buried at the churchyard. I checked with the priest a while back, and he said that would be fine. Could you make sure I'm buried next to Maud?"

"We can work that out. Don't worry anymore. Lay back and rest."

Whiskey laid his head back, closing his eyes, uttered his last words

"Thank you all. I love you."

Tears streamed down our cheeks, even Harold's. After endless hours of traveling with a knotted stomach, it was over in five minutes. Whiskey was gone. He breathed his last, even Billy knew it was over, and rested his little head on his master's chest.

Whiskey held on as he waited for my arrival. It occurred to me that this was the first time I had experienced that depth of feeling, even when I considered my own family. How strange and yet wonderful.

We lingered, suspended in time following Whiskey's passing, not ashamed of the tears. Harold came in and gently picked up Billy. He allowed him to lick the old man's reposed face and held the dog close to his chest. Billy didn't resist.

The first words any of them ever heard from Harold as he picked up the little dog were, "I'll t-take c-c-care of B-b-b-Billy and give him a g-good home." He turned and left as he lovingly stroked the trembling little head.

Arrangements were made, and Whiskey was buried next to Maud. Once I installed the headstone, we agreed to meet at the gravesite for a final goodbye.

When that day came, I drove to the cemetery and saw Janet's car parked beside the road. She wore a black dress and hat with black netting over her face, Brian in a black suit. Harold stood, wearing decent pants, his cockatoo on his shoulder, holding a leash with Billy on the end of it. I joined them. We discussed what a great guy Whiskey was and how we missed him. I reached down and picked up Billy. I scratched his ears. The little dog lovingly responded.

Brian motioned toward the grave, "You did a nice job on the headstone, Tony."

Then he read it aloud, "Jack Daniels. We called him Whiskey, a Dear

Friend of Dancing Diamond and Teddy Roosevelt."

I looked at Janet, "You like it, Janet?"

"Perfect," she responded.

We said our goodbyes. I walked to my car with Janet beside me. "What are you going to do now?" she asked.

I looked back at Whiskey's grave and thought, "I'm going to make something of myself."

She nodded and watched as I climbed into the Ford and started the engine.

CHAPTER 40

Lefty was having morning coffee as he read the paper. He turned to the personals section to check out the ads as usual. He saw an ad that interested him. It read, "Tony's Escort Service, Satisfaction Guaranteed," with a phone number underneath. Curious if this might be the same Tony he knew, he took a chance and dialed the number.

The phone rang, and in a sleepy voice, I answered, "Hello."

He recognized my voice, even with the sleepy tone. "Hey, Tone. This is Lefty. How are you doing, man? I haven't seen you in a while."

I perked up right as I recognized his voice. "Hey, Lefty, how are you doing? How did you find my number?"

"I found your ad in the paper and wondered if it was the same Tony."

"Oh, that. How are you doing?"

"I'm doing great. What say we get together for a drink?"

"Sure, that would be great. Where do you want to meet?"

"Let's say Tony Nic's down in North Beach. Can you get there around three this afternoon?"

"I'd love to see you."

At three o'clock, I parked my new red 1960 Corvette, with the top down, in front of Tony Nic's. I got out, smartly dressed, and entered the club. Lefty sat at the bar; I walked up and slapped him on the back.

"Hey, Tony," he said, getting up to hug me and pointing to the stool beside him. Have a seat!"

Jim, the bartender, asked, "What will you have?"

"I'll have a Jack Daniels on the rocks."

"Coming right up."

Lefty waited until I got my drink and asked, "Where are you living now?"

"I have a really nice place on the beach down from the Cliff House."

"That sounds cool. How long have you been down there?"

"A while now. Where are you living?" I asked.

"I got a flat in the Mission District."

"A lot of action there, I suppose?"

"It gets lively at times."

He cut to the chase, came right out, and asked, "Tell me about this escort business you have."

"It was an idea I had, so I put an ad in the paper."

"How's it working out?"

"The money is good, but sometimes I have to close my eyes," I laughed.

Lefty laughed with me, pushing his point, "How do you go about it?"

"Different ways. The best way is if my client comes to my house, I make a nice meal and have the place fixed up with dim lights and soft music. The women enjoy it."

"How do you get down to the REAL business?" Lefty asked.

"It's simple. Sometimes they have an event they don't want to attend alone, so we go out wherever she wants. On a nice evening, I'll take her for a walk on the beach and make her feel relaxed, comfortable, beautiful, and desirable. It's a nice evening out with no expectations. If nature takes its course, that's part of the deal."

Lefty never imagined such a thing, "You make them nice meals? Where do you get the recipes?"

"I hung out for a while with people seriously into cooking and picked up some stuff from them."

"I never thought of you as a guy who'd dig anything like that. Any special recipe that turns them on?"

"I have one that works well."

"What is it?"

I took a drink of Jack Daniels, "A Chili Relleno dish," I answered nonchalantly.

He blurted even more, confused and frustrated, "I've never heard of it. What is a chili relleno?"

After another swallow, "It's a Latin dish."

"How did you come up with that?"

My thoughts returned to Janet, Brian, Whiskey, Maud, Harold, and Maria. I lied and never told Brian and Janet the secret of Maria's chili relleno. I said she refused to give it up. Janet took it in stride and even apologized. She wanted to keep me hanging on for the next caper.

Maria treated me as a hero for healing her llamas, and I hung in with her because the sex was good.

I couldn't shake the feeling I was an appendage in her life and began to feel trapped. I knew one day we'd break off the relationship.

Unsurprisingly, Janet reached out to Maria and recruited her for the next caper in Spain. And no surprise Maria accepted, even after she knew Janet tried to trick her out of her secret. That was part of the game. In the end, the secret society felt more like a cult. I wasn't into cultish things.

Whiskey and Maud were the bright spots, but they were both gone. It was time to move on. I wouldn't explain this to Lefty; I kept it for myself.

I looked at Lefty out of the corner of my eye, and with a smirk, I lied, "I had to make love to a ninety-year-old woman to get that one."

He looked at me in shock, "You made love to a ninety-year-old woman to get a recipe?"

I nodded my head in affirmation.

"Oh my God!' Lefty gasped, "How was that?"

With a straight face, "It wasn't bad. I did have to keep waking her up."

Lefty looked up and began to laugh, "You have got to be shitting me!"

I looked straight ahead and took another drink.

Lefty took another drink, shook his head in disbelief, and wondered if he could pull off such a career.

"That sounds like a real gig. Do you think there is room for me?"

"Buy me another drink, and I'll think about it."

"Hey, Jim," Lefty shouted, "Another round here."

I took a long, slow, teasing sip for dramatic effect. Looking lefty straight in the eye, I said, "It's all a game, you know."

About the Author

Author Bob Means joined the Marines in the 1960s to escape a troubled childhood. Oblivious to the war in Vietnam, he was soon in the middle of combat, surviving two of the severest operations during the war (Operation Swift and the Tet Offensive). He returned home to struggle with his sanity, suffering from PTSD and an addiction to adrenaline. Bob found relief when he was invited to build an orphanage in Guatemala. This led to a thirty-year adventure as a shelter consultant in overseas disaster relief through a faith-based organization.

His fictional writing is inspired by his travels and the people he met, drawing on their experiences to create his stories. Although his writings are fiction, they are not far from the truth.

OTHER BOOKS BY BOB MEANS

My Soul to Keep, a Marine's Journal After Combat
Stealing Chili Relleno
The Adrian Account

PLEASE CONSIDER LEAVING A REVIEW

ON AMAZON